"Hey, are you with the Flirts?" the blond girl asked eagerly.

"Sometimes," Carrie replied, trying to sound in control.

"Well, like now?" the girl pressed. "Can you get us backstage?"

"They don't like fans coming backstage," Carrie said, which was true.

"We could be more than fans!" the brunette yelled, as Jay went into his hot solo on the keyboard. "We could be, like, up close and personal!"

"Oh, my God, look at his butt!" the blonde yelled.

Carrie turned. Billy was hopping to Jay's solo, his back to the audience.

"I swear, I just have to get him!" the blonde yelled.

Carrie couldn't take it anymore. "Well you can't," she snapped. "Because he's mine. . . ."

Sunset Illusions

CHERIE BENNETT

Sunset™ Island

SPLASH™

A BERKLEY / SPLASH BOOK

SUNSET ILLUSIONS is an original publication of
The Berkley Publishing Group.
This work has never appeared before in book form.

SUNSET ILLUSIONS

A Berkley Book / published by arrangement with
General Licensing Company, Inc.

PRINTING HISTORY
Berkley edition / August 1994

A GLC BOOK

Splash and *Sunset Island* are trademarks belonging to
General Licensing Company, Inc.

ISBN: 0-425-14336-8

BERKLEY®
Berkley Books are published by
The Berkley Publishing Group,
200 Madison Avenue, New York, New York 10016.
BERKLEY and the "B" design
are trademarks belonging to Berkley Publishing Corporation.

PRINTED IN THE UNITED STATES OF AMERICA

10 9 8 7 6 5 4 3 2 1

For my guy

ONE

"Yo, it's time for fun and games!" Samantha Bridges called, sitting up and brushing some sand off her knee. "Enough lying here in the sun, toasting our already toasty bodies!"

Her boyfriend, Presley Travis—better known as Pres—leaned up from the beach blanket and pulled on a handful of her red curls. "Come on back down here, darlin'," he drawled in a sexy Tennessee twang. "I was just about to fall asleep and have some wild dream about you and me."

"Why dream when you've got me next to you?" Sam asked, fluttering her eyelashes in an exaggerated fashion. "Anyway, I am the official social director for this afternoon—you guys promised—so the next event is—"

"Hold on!" Carrie Alden, Sam's best friend, interrupted her. "When did we make you social director?"

"When we voted this morning," Sam said innocently. "You mean you don't remember?"

"Nope," Carrie replied, pulling her sunglasses up into her hair so she could look at Sam.

"I don't either," Emma Cresswell, Sam's other best friend, agreed. "You made it up."

"True," Sam admitted. "But—"

"I'm too comfortable to move," Billy Sampson, Carrie's boyfriend, said blissfully. "You know how rare it is that I get to just hang out on the beach?"

"Yeah, like you musicians have such a tough life," Sam snorted. "Come on!" She jumped up, tugging the bottom half of her minuscule hot pink bikini back into place. "It's time for the second annual Sunset Island girl-on-his-shoulders guy-in-the-ocean chicken fights. Remember who won last year."

"You and Pres," Emma recalled, sitting up and crossing her slender legs. She adjusted the brim of her silk baseball cap to shade her face and pushed a strand of perfect blond hair off her face. "We heard about it every day for a week."

"Triumph knows no limits," Sam pontificated, taking a covered elastic band off her wrist and fastening her wild red hair on top of her head. "Now, who's in?"

"I'm game if you are," Jay Bailey told Emma.

Carrie caught Emma's eye. Last year Emma had been in the chicken fight with her boyfriend, Kurt Ackerman, she recalled. But they'd since broken up, and Kurt was gone, and Emma was still pretty devastated. Jay was a good guy—in fact, he was the keyboard player in the band they were in, Flirting With Danger, but there was nothing romantic going on between him and Emma, Carrie knew.

Carrie quickly squeezed Emma's hand, then she jumped up next to Sam. "No way are you winning again this year,

Bridges," she told Sam with mock ferocity.

Sam reached down and tugged on Pres's arm. "C'mon, Pres, we've got our honor to defend."

"I'm defendin' it right here on the beach," drawled Pres. He turned over and stretched his tanned, muscular arms over his head. "With the sun beating down on me. And there's nothin' you can do to stop me."

"I bet I can talk you into it," Sam joked. She knelt down and planted a soft kiss on Pres's right cheek.

"You might could win," Pres muttered with a grin. He took Sam's outstretched hand and allowed himself to be hoisted to his feet.

"Okay, Carrie," Sam commanded. "You and Billy have no choice."

"Hey, we need some ground rules this year," Carrie pointed out.

"You mean ocean rules," Sam corrected her.

"Whatever," Carrie said with a laugh. She adjusted the straps on her blue-and-white striped tank suit with the high-cut

4

legs. "All I know is that last year you left me with bruises on my bruises."

"You are courage free," Sam declared. "Besides, I'm reformed. I couldn't hurt a fly."

"How about one couple on one couple, winner takes on me and Carrie?" Billy suggested.

"But Pres and I are the champs, winner should take us on!" Sam exclaimed.

Billy pulled Carrie back down on the blanket and nuzzled her neck. "I can't hear you, Sam," he called up to her.

"They want to be alone," Emma translated for Sam.

"Well, why didn't they just say so?" Sam groused. "Last one in the water has to buy dinner!" Sam yelled, and she ran for the ocean. Emma, Pres, and Jay ran after her.

"Alone at last," Billy said, kissing Carrie on her shoulder.

"Nice," Carrie commented with a smile. She lay down next to Billy and closed her eyes to the hot Sunset Island sun. For the moment, she felt totally content. She was nineteen years old and for the second summer in a row she had a job as an au pair on one of the most beautiful resort islands in the world, Sunset Island, off the coast of Maine. Her two best friends, Emma and Sam, were on the island with her. And she was totally in love with Billy Sampson, the sweetest, smartest, nicest, cutest guy she'd ever met in her life. Not only that, but he was the lead singer for Flirting With Danger—or the Flirts, as they were more commonly known.

Zillions of girls are after him, Carrie thought to herself with satisfaction, *but Billy loves straightforward, girl-next-door, non-makeup-wearing me.*

Billy kissed Carrie again. She smiled and turned on to her back, settling into a comfortable position. It was amazing, really, how wonderful her life was at just that moment. Never before had she had two best friends like Emma and Sam. And it was funny, really, because all three of them were so different.

Sam, the tall, thin redheaded flirt with the wild hair, came from the tiny farming town of Junction, Kansas. She'd dropped out of college early in her freshman year to become a dancer at Disney World, but then she'd been fired for being "too original." Her greatest ambition in the world was to live the lifestyle of the rich and famous.

Then there was petite, beautiful, blond-haired Emma, who was one of the richest heiresses in the country. Her blue-blood mother had raised her to be a total snob, and she'd been educated in Europe at the finest boarding schools. But Emma hadn't turned out how her mother wanted at all. She wasn't a snob, and she'd decided to take a job as an au pair the summer before and work for a living (much to her mother's horror), and in fact her great dream was to join the Peace Corps and work with primates in Africa.

And then there's me, Carrie thought sleepily. *I'm just an upper-middle-class girl from New Jersey with normal brown hair and normal brown eyes and the full figure I inherited from my mother. I know I'm smart, and I love being a student at Yale, and people seem to like my photographs but I don't think of myself as being very spectacular.* She opened her eyes and glanced over at Billy, and she smiled. *But I guess Billy loves me just the way I am.*

Carrie felt Billy's hand on the sun-kissed skin of her shoulder. "Hey," he said, "need some more sunblock?"

"I don't think so," Carrie replied. "You just put some on my back a half hour ago."

"Well, how about if I just give you a back rub and pretend, then?" Billy asked. She rolled over and he ran his hand firmly over Carrie's back, kneading the skin gently.

"Mmmm, that feels great," she murmured.

"Do you know how cute you look lying there?" he asked her softly.

"No," Carrie replied seriously. "I think you should tell me."

Billy laughed. "On a cuteness scale of one to ten, you are an eleven."

She smiled. "You really think that?"

"You know I do." He leaned over and kissed her softly on the lips. "There's only one problem."

"What's that?" Carrie asked.

"I would really like to be alone with you right now instead of out here on this beach, waiting to let Sam and Pres kick our butts in a chicken fight."

"We could sneak off," Carrie suggested. "You know, just kind of disappear."

Billy tickled her quickly in the ribs. "I know you better than that. You're much too nice to just disappear on your friends."

"That's me," Carrie said lightly. "I'm just the nicest girl."

Billy stopped rubbing Carrie's back and cocked his head to one side. "You really are, you know," he said.

Carrie sat up. "Nice?" Billy nodded and Carrie wrinkled her nose. "Nice is so . . . boring, isn't it?"

"You are definitely not boring," Billy asserted. "You're one of a kind. I mean, even my family would like you, and they don't like anyone!"

Carrie raised her eyebrows. "You never told me that before."

Billy fiddled with the stud in his earlobe. "Yeah, well, it's not such a happy topic of conversation," he admitted.

"You don't get along with your parents?" Carrie asked him.

Billy shrugged. "They weren't too thrilled about my becoming a musician. My dad owns an auto body repair business in Seattle—it belonged to his dad before him—and I guess he always hoped either me or my older brother, Evan, would take over the family business."

"So, where's Evan now?" Carrie asked gently, hugging her knees with her arms. She had asked Billy about his family in the past, but he had always been reluctant to talk very much about them.

"In the air force," Billy explained. "He's a real straight arrow. You know, military haircut, military bearing, and all that."

Carrie tugged playfully on Billy's ponytail. "And then there's you."

"Yeah, me," Billy echoed ruefully. "The family rebel."

"Do your parents know how much talent you have?" Carrie asked him softly.

Billy shrugged. "That kind of thing is lost on them."

"But if they knew how really talented you are—"

"It wouldn't matter," Billy interrupted. "Listen, you have great parents, Car. I mean, I've met them, and they're terrific. But everyone's parents aren't like that."

"I guess I'm lucky, huh," Carrie said.

"Yeah," Billy agreed. "We'll have to add that to your list of virtues."

"Oh, well," Carrie said breezily, "just call me Saint Carrie."

"Believe me," Billy said huskily, leaning over to kiss Carrie again, "I definitely do *not* think of you as a saint."

"Hey, is my back burned?" Sam asked as she, Carrie, and Emma strolled down the boardwalk later that evening.

The guys had a song-writing session planned, and the girls had the evening free to hang out together.

Emma walked behind Sam and peered at her back, bare in her low-cut sundress. "Yes," Emma replied. "I told you to put on more sunblock."

"But I have a tan already!" Sam protested. "How can you get burned over a tan?"

"By not using sunblock," Carrie said, "which I've told you only ten thousand times." She reached into her purse for some cherry lip balm and spread it on her lips.

"Oh, well," Sam said breezily, "I believe in living dangerously. Hey, what do you guys think of this dress?" She spun around in a circle and the full skirt of her sundress danced around her knees. It was strapless, with a low-cut back, in a polished cotton material featuring a flower print in red, pink, and purple. With it she wore her usual trademark red cowboy boots.

"Very cute," Carrie commented.

"And very conservative for you, I might add," Emma said.

"Isn't it?" Sam agreed. "I don't know, it just appealed to me. Oh, well, you know what I say, always keep 'em guessing!"

"So, where did you get it?" Emma wondered.

"The Cheap Boutique, where else?" Sam

replied. "The two of you are looking particularly cute tonight, too, by the way."

Carrie looked over at Emma, who had on baggy white linen pants and a cropped white linen top. She knew that although the outfit looked deceptively simple, it had probably been very expensive. Then she looked down at her own jeans and red checked western shirt. *Oh, well,* Carrie thought, *so I'm not a fashion maverick. At least I'm comfortable.*

"Did I tell you guys that the Cheap Boutique has sold three of my original Samstyles dresses already?" Sam asked excitedly.

Sam had recently begun her own business, designing dresses that were draped, and held together with rhinestone pins. She was being commissioned by the owner of the Cheap Boutique. As she had explained to her friends, since she couldn't sew at all she had resorted to draping and pinning fabric.

"That's so terrific!" Carrie cried. "Wow, you're really in business!"

"Well, your Sunset Magic perfume is selling so well, I had to do something in self-defense," Sam replied. She sniffed Carrie's hair. "You're wearing it now, right?"

Carrie nodded. "I love it. It smells just like summer to me."

"Oh, save it for the ad campaign," Sam snorted. "Hey, let's get some cotton candy!"

Sam ran ahead to the cotton-candy stand, Emma and Carrie ambling slowly along behind her.

"Does someone feed her high-energy pills or something?" Carrie asked Emma as they sauntered along.

"She claims it's in the water in Kansas," Emma replied with a smile.

"So . . . did you have fun this afternoon?" Carrie asked Emma.

Emma nodded. "It was nice."

Carrie looked at her. "But not the same . . . as before, I mean."

"No, not the same," Emma agreed.

They walked a few more steps in silence.

"I got another letter from Kurt," Emma finally said.

"What did he say?"

Emma shrugged daintily and pushed a

strand of hair behind her pearl-studded ear. "It was newsy, breezy, all about Michigan and some dune-bike race his cousins were in."

After Kurt and Emma had broken up, Kurt had left the island—the island he loved, the island that had always been his home—so he wouldn't have to face the pain of running into Emma. He was staying with cousins in Michigan, and he planned to try to get into the Air Force Academy in the fall.

"Nothing personal?" Carrie wondered.

Emma shook her head no. "I keep feeling as if he wants to say things to me but he's not." She sighed heavily. "But maybe that's just my imagination."

"Well, it makes sense," Carrie allowed. "I mean, when he was on the island and you ran into him on the beach, he told you he still cares—"

"But he's still so angry that he can't say anything personal," Emma finished. "I know." She sighed again. "I guess he probably has mixed emotions, just like I do."

"Have you heard from Adam?" Carrie asked.

Adam Briarly was Sam's half brother, and he and Emma had met and become attracted to each other earlier in the summer. Adam lived in Los Angeles.

"He called me yesterday," Emma said. "He finished writing his screenplay."

"That's great!"

"He said he's sending it to me," Emma explained. "He wants my opinion—not that I know anything about screenplays."

"I have a feeling it's good," Carrie said. "There's just something about Adam—"

"I know," Emma agreed. She gave a small, rueful laugh. "In the movies it always looks so wonderful to have two incredible guys in your life—"

"It's Sam's idea of perfection," Carrie said.

"Not mine," Emma replied. "I just feel . . . mixed up. Confused. Anxious."

"Caught between Kurt and Adam," Carrie translated.

Emma nodded. "I hate it. I really do."

"Hey, you guys have to taste this cotton candy," Sam said, running back over to them with a huge pink concoction on a stick. She pulled off a wad and let it melt on her tongue.

"No, thanks," Emma said.

"You don't know what you're missing," Sam insisted. "My parents never let me have this stuff when I was a kid." She pulled off another hunk and popped it into her mouth. "They said it was pure sugar and it would rot my teeth."

"They were probably right," Carrie agreed.

"Please," Sam said. "I can't give up sugar. I mean, I have no vices. I don't drink, I don't do drugs, and I'm a virgin. I need all the sugar I can get!"

Emma laughed. "Gee, since you put it like that . . ." She reached for a hunk of the cotton candy herself.

"Do you think maybe sugar is, like, a substitute for sex?" Sam asked. Her eyes strayed to two cute guys in Harvard sweatshirts jogging by in the opposite direction. "Whoa, babe-alicious to the max!" She turned around and watched the guys jog away.

"Down, girl," Carrie commanded, turning Sam back around.

"Maybe I should just finally do it with Pres so I won't salivate every time a fine guy jogs by," Sam mused. She ate the last of her cotton candy and threw the white paper cone into the nearest trash barrel.

"I don't think that's the best reason that I've ever heard to have sex for the first time," Emma replied.

They sat on a nearby bench and stared out at the ocean.

"Well, maybe I'm ready to do it," Sam said. "You know, just because I want to."

"Really?" Emma asked, staring at her friend.

Sam shrugged. "I'm not sure."

"So then you should wait," Emma said firmly.

"I don't know," Sam replied. "Maybe if you and Kurt had actually done the horizontal boogie you wouldn't have broken up."

"That is really dumb," Carrie said. "They broke up because Emma wasn't ready to get married."

"I'm really glad we didn't do it," Emma

said softly. "I mean, it would be so much harder, now that we've split up, if we'd been sleeping together. . . ." She stared out at the darkened ocean. "Lately I've been thinking, about virginity and everything—"

"You mean you've been thinking about sex," Sam corrected her, "my favorite topic next to food."

"No, I mean virginity," Emma said. "I've been thinking that maybe . . . well, maybe I want to be a virgin when I get married."

Both of her friends stared at her.

"Run that by me again?" Sam suggested.

"Maybe it's a good thing," Emma continued earnestly. "It's certainly romantic."

"Yeah, but what if you marry some guy and then the two of you turn out to be totally sexually incompatible?" Sam said. "What do you do then?"

"But Kurt and I were perfect together," Emma murmured.

"Hel-lo!" Sam called. "You and Kurt are kaput, finito, over."

"They're writing to each other," Carrie reminded Sam.

"I just can't believe you'd want to be a virgin when you get married," Sam marveled, ignoring Carrie's remark. "Are you serious?"

"I don't know," Emma admitted. "It's just something that I'm thinking about. I mean, if you're going to marry the one great love of your life, doesn't it make sense to start being true to him even before you meet him?"

"Get me the hurl bag," Sam declared.

"Yeah, you talk so tough," Carrie teased her. "But just remember you're the one who declared yourself the oldest living virgin in the United States."

"Well, it's not a title I'm proud of," Sam said haughtily. She thought a moment. "Well, maybe I am. But don't tell anyone."

Emma looked over at Carrie. "It's been quite a while since you and Billy took those AIDS tests. Are you still planning to be together?"

"Yes," Carrie said quietly. "I really love

Billy, and he loves me. We've been together for a long time, we're totally committed—"

"You've got to take videos so I know what to do when I take the big plunge myself!" Sam cried.

Emma poked her in the ribs.

"We've been talking about getting a room at the Sunset Inn," Carrie continued. "It feels kind of funny, planning it all out and everything. . . ."

"That's better than pretending you're just swept up in the moment and not using birth control or protection against HIV," Emma pointed out.

"God, life used to be much more romantic than this," Sam sighed. "I should have been a teenager during the sixties— free love and all that—"

"You probably still would have been the oldest living virgin in the northern hemisphere," Carrie teased her.

Sam thought about it. "Yeah, probably," she admitted. She sighed dramatically, then she jumped up. "Listen, I have to run back to the food stand. I may have to eat two more cotton candies to get over this!"

TWO

"We're going to the park!" five-year-old Chloe cried to her thirteen-year-old brother, Ian.

"Big wow," Ian muttered, slumping over on the couch in the Templetons' family room. He fitted the earphones that were around his neck onto his ears and turned up the volume of his Walkman.

It was the next day, and Carrie was about to take Chloe to a nearby park that had all kinds of huge Day-Glo-colored rubber structures for little kids to climb on. It was one of Chloe's favorite places.

"I think Chloe needs a sweater," Claudia Templeton said. "It's kind of cool out."

Carrie worked for Claudia and Graham Templeton, or, as he was more commonly known, Graham Perry. Yes, *the* Graham Perry—one of the most famous rock stars of all time. At first she'd been totally awed to be working for someone so famous, but now, in her second summer working for Graham and Claudia, she really considered them friends as well as employers.

"I already got it," Carrie said with a smile, picking up the little girl's sweater from the couch. She had to move Ian to get to it. Ian scowled and turned his music up louder.

"Well, he's in a foul mood," Claudia commented, leaning against the doorframe.

"Girl trouble," Carrie informed her. She turned to Chloe. "Okay, little one," she said, "you ready to rock and roll?"

"Where's Sam?" Chloe asked as Carrie helped her on with her sweater.

"She's meeting us at the park," Carrie explained.

"I love Sam," Chloe said happily.

"Me, too," Carrie agreed.

"Could you pick up a couple of pizzas for dinner on your way home?" Claudia asked Carrie. "That way neither one of us will have to cook."

"Sure," Carrie agreed, scooping up the car keys to Claudia's new Fiat from the table. She walked over to Ian and moved one of his earphones. "We're having a pizza for dinner," she said loudly. "What do you want on it?"

"I don't care," Ian said with a scowl, quickly replacing his earphone.

Carrie shrugged, took Chloe's hand, and headed for the front door. Claudia followed her.

"He's been in a terrible mood for days," Claudia commented.

"I know," Carrie agreed.

"So, what did you mean about girl trouble?"

I have to be careful here, Carrie thought. *I don't want to tell Claudia anything that Ian wouldn't tell her himself.*

"Why don't you ask him," Carrie suggested.

Claudia pushed some hair off her face and looked irritated. "That's just the point. He never tells me anything. I'm his mother. That's why I'm asking you."

"Well, he's having a little trouble with Becky right now," Carrie admitted.

Becky Jacobs was Ian's girlfriend. She was also one of the twins in Sam's charge. Becky and Ian had been an item for a while, but lately Becky seemed to be cooling off toward him, and Ian was really upset about it.

"He's too young to have a girlfriend," Claudia pronounced, folding her arms.

"He doesn't think so," Carrie said gently.

Claudia laughed. "What am I saying? I can't even believe those words just popped out of my mouth. I was totally boy crazy at thirteen."

"What does boy crazy mean?" Chloe asked, wide-eyed.

"It means something your father will never let you be," Claudia replied, kneeling down to hug her daughter. She stood up and smiled. "I swear, these rockers are the worst when it comes to their own kids. Graham probably won't let Chloe date until she's thirty." She ruffled her daughter's hair.

26

"Come on, Carrie, let's go," Chloe said, tugging on her au pair's hand.

"Have fun," Claudia called as Carrie and Chloe headed outside.

It took them no time at all to arrive at the nearby park, where Sam was already waiting on a bench, her face lifted to the warm afternoon sun.

"Girlfriend!" Chloe yelled, running over to Sam.

"Girlfriend!" Sam cried back, holding out her arms to Chloe.

Chloe jumped into them, hugging Sam hard. "How are you, girlfriend?" she asked.

"You never should have taught her to say that," Carrie said with a laugh.

"But she's so cute," Sam replied. She turned to Chloe. "So, what's up? How many dates did you have this week?"

"Mommy says Daddy won't let me date until I'm thirty," Chloe replied solemnly.

"Bummer," Sam commented.

"Wanna come on the jungle gym with me?" Chloe asked Sam hopefully.

"In a few minutes," Sam promised. "I want to talk to Carrie first, okay?"

"Okay," Chloe agreed. "Bye, girlfriend!" she added, running off.

"You've created a monster," Carrie said, sitting down next to Sam.

"To know me is to love me," Sam sang out.

"I can't believe you actually got here before us."

"I'm turning over a new leaf," Sam declared. "I'm not going to be late anymore."

"Good for you," Carrie approved.

Sam leaned back and put her hands behind her head. "This is the life, huh? I'm telling you, since the monsters started working as counselors-in-training at Club Sunset Island, I've actually had free time on my hands."

"Not me," Carrie said, reaching down to pluck a dandelion from the grass. "In fact, Claudia and Graham are going to New York next week, so I'll be chained to the homefront. I'm lucky they're letting me go hear the Flirts at the Play Café tomorrow night."

"Isn't that going to make things a little tough on you and Billy?" Sam wondered.

Carrie shrugged. "We always find a way to see each other. Anyway, he's pretty busy too."

"Hey, we're not talking just about seeing each other here," Sam reminded her. "I mean, according to what you told me and Emma last night, you are about to see *all* of each other, if you catch my drift."

"Consider it caught," Carrie said dryly.

Sam turned to Carrie. "So, are you guys really gonna Do It?"

A small smile came to Carrie's lips.

"Does that Mona Lisa grin mean yes?" Sam pressed.

"It means . . . I'm thinking about it," Carrie replied slowly.

"I swear, you've put more thought into this than went into writing the Bible—both Testaments," Sam groused. "What I'm looking for here is dirt."

Carrie wriggled her eyebrows at Sam. "I'll never tell."

Sam leaned closer. "Yes, you will. Because you love me and you know my life is hopelessly dull, so I need to glom on to yours."

"Hey, you and Pres are back together! I wouldn't call that dull!"

"That's true," Sam said. "So, are you gonna, like, just go into a drugstore and buy condoms?"

"That sounds reasonable," Carrie said.

"I hate it when you get all mature," Sam declared. "You mean to tell me you won't be embarrassed to ask for condoms at Sunset Drugs?"

"Nope."

Sam stared at her a minute. "You're such a liar!" she finally shrieked.

"You're right!" Carrie admitted, laughing, too.

"Maybe you should just ask Billy to get some," Sam said.

"No," Carrie said firmly. "If I'm going to do it, I'm going to take responsibility for it. I mean, you can't just depend on the guy."

"Amen," Sam agreed.

"Hey, girlfriend!" Chloe yelled from the jungle gym. "Look at me!" She hung upside down, her knees wrapped around the bar, and scratched her armpits like a monkey. Fortunately there was a thick rubber mat below her, so Carrie wasn't too worried about her getting hurt.

"You're fabulous!" Sam called back to the little girl.

"She really is great, isn't she," Carrie agreed, smiling fondly at Chloe.

"Yeah, very cute kid," Sam said. "Of course, I wouldn't think she was so cute if she were mine."

"Oh, you would, too," Carrie said. "You'd be crazy for her."

"No kids for this babe," Sam said adamantly.

"But you'd be a really good mother!" Carrie protested.

"*Moi?*" Sam asked. "Please! I can't even handle the twins, and they're already fourteen!"

"I'd love to have a little girl like Chloe," Carrie mused, watching the child as she scampered over to a swing.

"Well, one thing is for sure," Sam said. "You and Billy would have a gorgeous kid."

"Can you imagine a little boy that

looked just like Billy?" Carrie said with a sigh.

"Drooling, puking, filling his diaper," Sam continued in a dreamy voice. "Oh, so darling."

"But babies are so sweet!" Carrie protested.

"Good, have twenty. I'd rather have a zillion boyfriends and a mountain of cash."

"How about one guy you really, truly love and want to spend the rest of your life with?" Carrie asked.

"How about Johnny Depp in a water bed?" Sam countered.

"I'm serious!"

"Oh, how do I know?" Sam asked. "I mean, I can't even figure out what I'm doing in the fall, much less with the rest of my life." She stood up and stretched her long arms. "What happens with you and Billy in the fall anyway?"

"Well, I'll be back at Yale—"

"Long-distance love?" Sam questioned dubiously.

"It's not too far from Sunset Island,"

Carrie said. "And Billy will come and visit me at school all the time—"

"I don't know . . ." Sam began.

"I do." Carrie stood up. "Billy and I really and truly love each other. We're completely committed. This isn't some . . . summer fling. It's forever."

"Forever forever?"

Carrie raised her eyebrows. "Is there another kind?"

"Sure," Sam replied. "There's we-just-think-it's-forever-because-we're-overcome-by-lust and then there's real forever."

"We have the second kind," Carrie said firmly. "How about you and Pres?"

"Who knows?" Sam said with a sigh. "I mean, I know I love him and I want to be with him. But is it forever? What if it's just that I want to jump his bones and kiss him until his lips fall off?"

"Hey, you girlfriends!" Chloe called, running over to them. "Come on the merry-go-round with me!"

"We've been beckoned," Carrie said.

"Last one to the merry-go-round eats chocolate-covered ants!" Sam yelled. "Go!"

She and Carrie took off, pretending to run fast but letting Chloe get ahead of them.

Chloe laughed and ran toward the merry-go-round, triumphantly beating both of them.

Ring-ring-ring!

"Templeton residence, this is Carrie," Carrie said, answering the phone in the kitchen. She'd just finished loading the dishwasher with the plates from the pizza and salad, and she turned it on as she held the phone in the crook of her neck.

"Hi, it's me," came Emma's voice.

"Hi, what's up?" She grabbed a sponge from the sink and began to wipe down the kitchen table.

"I just got the strangest phone call," Emma said softly.

"From whom?"

Chloe came running into the kitchen. "Carrie, Ian won't let me watch TV with him!" she whined.

"Hold on a sec, Em," Carrie said into

the phone. She turned to Chloe. "Why not, honey?"

"He says it's MTV and I'm too young," Chloe answered, pouting.

"Well, he's right," Carrie agreed. "Why don't you ask him if the two of you can watch something else."

"But I like MTV!" Chloe cried. "I like Salt 'N' Pepa!"

Carrie shook her head ruefully. *It is impossible to keep a little kid a little kid today,* she thought. "I'll tell you what," she told Chloe, "when I get off the phone, I'll read you a story, okay?"

"Okay," Chloe said reluctantly, and she scuffed her sneakers against the floor tile as she slowly left the kitchen.

"Sorry, Em," Carrie said, throwing the sponge in the sink. "Chloe and Ian aren't getting along very well lately. Ian is in a funk over Becky and he's taking it out on everyone."

"Did they break up?" Emma asked.

"Sam says she has a date with some guy from something called Camp Eagle on Eagle Island," Carrie explained. "I don't know much about it, and Ian isn't talking. So, what about this strange phone call of yours?" She sat down at the kitchen table.

"It was Adam," Emma said.

"So, why is that strange?"

"He sounded . . . I don't know . . . odd," Emma said softly.

"Odd how?"

"Like . . . look, I know this is probably crazy, but he sounded so hyper. Like maybe he had taken something."

"You mean speed?" Carrie asked with surprise.

"I know how crazy that sounds," Emma said again. "I mean, Adam told me he's totally against drugs. . . ."

"Maybe it was just caffeine," Carrie suggested. "You know, too much coffee."

"Maybe," Emma agreed. "He said he hadn't mailed me his screenplay yet because at the last minute he figured out what the problems were in the second act and he stayed up all night to fix them."

"So it probably is caffeine, then," Carrie said. "He must have drank a pot of coffee to stay up and write."

"I guess I'm overreacting," Emma said. "He said this screenplay means everything to him."

"Everything?"

"Actually he said I'd mean even more than the screenplay to him if I'd let it happen," Emma admitted.

"But you're still confused," Carrie acknowledged. "Listen, it's really okay, you know. You don't have to choose between Adam and Kurt right now."

"Or ever, probably," Emma added. "It's not like Kurt has given me any indication at all that there's a future for us."

Carrie got up and got the broom from the closet and began to sweep the floor, still holding the phone in the crook of her neck. "Do you want a future with him?"

Emma sighed deeply. "Honestly, Carrie, I don't know. When I talk to Adam, I think about Kurt. And when I write to Kurt, I think about Adam. I'm a wreck."

"Yes, but you're a nice wreck," Carrie said.

"Thanks for that," Emma sighed. "Anyway, since tomorrow is Sunday, Adam is overnighting the screenplay to me on Monday, and I'll have it on Tuesday."

"Happy reading."

"He told me he isn't going to be able to sleep until I read it and tell him what I think," Emma told her.

"Well, I guess he really values your opinion." She moved the chairs from the table so that she could sweep underneath.

"I suppose I should just be flattered," Emma agreed.

"You don't sound flattered." She reached into the closet for the dustpan.

"I am," Emma insisted. "It's just that . . . oh, look, I'm probably making something out of nothing. I just thought he sounded really strange. Manic. But maybe it's in my head."

"I guess you'll just have to see how he sounds the next time you talk to him," Carrie said logically. "Or you could ask him if he's doing drugs or something."

"No, I couldn't do that," Emma said

quickly. "I'm sure you're right. It's nothing."

"Carrie!" Chloe called, running into the kitchen. "Mommy says I can have ice cream!"

"I have to go," Carrie said. "Are you okay?"

"Oh, sure," Emma assured her. "I just hope his screenplay is good, that's all. The last thing he said to me was 'Emma, I desperately want you to think it's great, because it's my heart on paper.'"

"Wow," Carrie breathed. "That's a lot of pressure."

"Carrie!" Chloe whined.

"I really have to go," Carrie told Emma. "I'll call you later." She hung up the phone and headed for the freezer to get Chloe her ice cream, and just then the phone rang again.

"Templeton residence, Carrie speaking."

"Hey, did I mention that I love you?" came a deep male voice through the phone line.

Carrie smiled. "How many guesses do I

get to figure out who this is," she said softly. Ian walked into the kitchen and opened the fridge to get a Coke.

"You'd better know," came Billy's reply.

"I want a Coke, too," Chloe told her brother.

"Too bad," he replied, popping it open.

"I do know," Carrie said into the phone. "And I feel the same way."

"Meaning that you can't say it because someone is there," Billy surmised.

"Two someones, actually," Carrie explained.

"Gotcha," Billy said. "Well, I just wanted you to know I was thinking about you, and I can't wait until tomorrow night when I can see that cute mug of yours again."

Carrie hung up, feeling chill bumps of happiness all up and down her spine.

"Can I please have ice cream now?" Chloe asked, her little hands on her hips, as if to say that her patience with Carrie was truly coming to an end. Ian didn't speak to her at all; he just left the room.

"Two scoops," Carrie promised her.

I am so lucky, she thought blissfully. *I don't have to try to decide between two guys like Emma, I'm not afraid of love like Sam, and I have the greatest guy on the face of the earth.*

Nothing can possibly go wrong. Nothing.

THREE

"Answer me this," Erin Kane said, fiddling with the star-shaped rhinestone pin at her waist that held together her new Samstyles stage outfit. "What if I inhale to go for a high note and this pin pops?"

Sam grinned at her in the dressing room mirror. "Then I hope you wore cute underwear."

"How about if you double-pin it underneath the brooch?" Emma suggested, handing Erin a safety pin. "That's what I did."

Erin gratefully took the safety pin, Sam fluffed her wild hair in the mirror, and Emma sprayed on some Sunset Magic perfume as Carrie snapped away with her camera.

It was the next night, and the girls were backstage at the Play Café, waiting to perform with the Flirts. This would be only the second time they were performing publicly since Erin Kane had replaced Diana De Witt as the third backup singer-dancer. Everyone in the band was really happy about Erin, and even happier to see the last of Diana.

"Does this thing make me look flat-chested?" Sam asked, scrutinizing her image in the mirror. Like Emma and Erin, she wore a Samstyles fashion, draped, tucked, and pinned. The first outfits she'd done for them had all been in black velvet. These new ones were all tie-dyed pastel cotton. Sam's was white with shades of pink wrapped around and around under the bustline.

"Well, you're not big-busted," Erin said good-naturedly, fastening the extra safety pins at her waist.

"Oh, thank you," Sam said, "that is so helpful. You fill me with confidence right before I go onstage."

"But, Sam, you're gorgeous and have the figure of a fashion model," Erin said with a laugh. "You can't actually expect me to feel sorry for you."

Carrie clicked off shots of Erin and Sam as they bantered back and forth. *They're both great looking,* Carrie thought, *even though Erin probably weighs sixty pounds more than Sam.* Erin was a curvy, full-figured size eighteen, and Sam was all long legs and angles, a size eight if it ran small.

"How's your dad feeling, Erin?" Carrie asked as she put a new roll of film into her camera.

Recently there had been a fire at the new club Surf's Up, just as the girls were about to give the big kickoff party for their perfume, Sunset Magic. Erin's dad had gotten caught in the storeroom and had suffered serious burns.

"He's better all the time," Erin told her. She shook some of her long blond hair off her face. "I'll tell you what has helped the most. It's the whole thing with Sunset Magic. I mean, no matter what kind of pain he's in, he looks forward to hearing

45

progress reports from you guys about the perfume."

"We never, ever could have done it without him," Emma said. "He has to know that."

"I think he does," Erin agreed thoughtfully. "One of his goals right now is to be well enough to get out of the hospital rehab and into the stores so he can see with his own two eyes how the perfume is doing."

"When are we going to be able to visit him?" Carrie asked.

"I'll let you know," Erin promised. "He really has appreciated your cards and flowers. You wouldn't believe all the mail he's been getting! Like he got this huge card from . . . what's it called—it's initials, some island organization for some kind of ethics. . . ."

"That would be COPE," Sam replied. "It's stands for Citizens of Positive Ethics. How do they know your dad?"

"They don't, as far as I know," Erin said with a shrug.

"They have a committee," Emma explained. "When anything bad happens to anyone who lives on the island, the committee sends a card. They look at the entire island as a family."

"Well, they sure haven't treated you like family," Sam pointed out.

Kurt had been very active in COPE, and when Emma and Kurt had broken up, it seemed as if everyone in COPE blamed Emma for breaking Kurt's heart.

"I hope there aren't a lot of people from COPE here tonight," Emma said quietly, putting her perfume back into her purse.

Carrie touched Emma's arm lightly. "I think they must be over all that taking-sides stuff about you and Kurt by now."

"I doubt it," Emma said honestly. She gave a small laugh, but her eyes looked sad. "Can you imagine what they'd do if Kurt and I ever got back together again?"

"They'd have to knock Kurt right off that pedestal they keep him on," Sam said, fishing her lipstick out of her purse.

"You guys are on in five," Linda Cabrillo, the new Play Café house manager said, sticking her head in the door.

"Thanks," Erin called back to her. She

put her hands on her stomach. "I just got nervous."

"Everyone ready?" Billy asked from the doorway.

"Why do I get so nervous?" Erin asked no one in particular.

Carrie walked over to Billy and kissed him softly. "That's for luck."

"You can give me that kind of luck anytime," Billy told her, kissing her back.

"Please, no mush before show time," Sam decreed, fiddling with the earring in her left ear. "It's my new rule."

"You wouldn't be saying that if Pres stuck his head in here," Billy teased her.

"Well, as we all know, Sam is the exception to every rule," Erin explained.

Billy laughed. "She sure has your number!" He gave Carrie a quick hug, pulling her close. "How about we spend some time alone tonight?" he whispered in her ear.

"I'd love that," she agreed, smiling at him.

He kissed her again. "Okay, guys, let's boogie!" he called.

Carrie stayed in the dressing room

until they'd all left for the stage, then she took the other door, which led into the main area of the club. There was already a huge crowd around the stage and an expectant buzz in the air. The Flirts were the up-and-coming hometown band, and always drew a big crowd. It seemed as if most of the island had come out to hear them.

"Hey, everybody having fun?" Linda Cabrillo yelled into the microphone. She was tall and thin, with short, straight black hair and intense brown eyes. Carrie thought she looked like a tall Winona Ryder.

"Yeahhhh!" the crowd roared expectantly.

"Well, tonight we have a band I haven't heard yet," Linda admitted.

"We have!" someone yelled, and everyone cheered and whistled.

"Yeah, I've heard these guys are the best," Linda agreed. "So please welcome your homeboys and girls . . . Flirting With Danger!"

The crowd went wild, and the Flirts ran onto the stage.

"It's great to be back at the Play Café," Billy said into the mike. "We hope you've all met the two newest members of our band, our drummer Jake Fisher, and our new backup singer, Erin Kane! Take a bow, you two!"

Carrie clicked away as Erin and Jake bowed and waved to the audience. Billy had introduced them recently at a special COPE fund-raiser on the island, but there hadn't been nearly as many people there as were present at the Play Café this night.

"We'd like to start out with a little tune we call 'Love Junkie'," Billy said, and as Jake counted off the beat, the crowd went wild, since they all knew the tune.

Carrie used her zoom lens as Billy sang his heart out, snapping away at his face, his torso, catching the sexy curve of his arm as he raised it high above his head.

"That guy is too hot!" she heard a girl next to her scream to her friend.

"I want him so bad!" the other girl screeched, grabbing her friend's arm. "Can we get backstage?"

"Yeah, I know Linda!" the first girl yelled over the music.

Carrie turned to look at them, a hot flush of anger crawling across her face. The blond one was wearing a flower-print bra top and the teeniest, tiniest of cutoff jeans. The curly-haired brunette was wearing a little flowered minidress that barely covered her panties. And no bra.

For just a moment Carrie wanted to scream that she was Billy's girlfriend, and she wanted to slap both of them silly. But she stopped herself. *I don't need to feel so defensive,* Carrie told herself. *Girls like this are after Billy all the time. And he never responds. At least I don't think he does.*

"Hey, does he have a girlfriend?" the first girl screamed to the second.

"Who cares?" the second girl yelled back.

Don't get upset, Carrie cautioned herself. Even though she felt like bopping both girls over the head with her camera, instead, she turned to them and began snapping their photos. They vamped for her, dancing around, pouting and posing.

"Hey, are you with the Flirts?" the blonde asked eagerly.

"Sometimes," Carrie replied, trying to sound in control.

"Well, like now?" the girl pressed. "Can you get us backstage?"

"They don't like fans coming backstage," Carrie said, which was true.

"We could be more than fans!" the brunette yelled as Jay went into his hot solo on the keyboard. "We could be, like, up close and personal!"

"Oh, my God, look at his butt!" the blonde yelled.

Carrie turned. Billy was bopping to Jay's solo, his back to the audience.

"I swear, I just have to get him!" the blonde yelled.

Carrie couldn't take it anymore. "Well, you can't," she snapped. "Because he's mine."

The two girls stopped jumping around and stared at Carrie. "Billy is *yours*?" the brunette asked, wide-eyed.

"He's my boyfriend," Carrie qualified.

The two girls traded looks, then looked back at Carrie again. "You?" the blonde finally said dubiously. Her eyes scanned Carrie up and down. Carrie had on baggy jeans and a denim shirt tied at her waist. She didn't have on any makeup, and her hair was tied up in a ponytail. Clearly she didn't really believe that Carrie was going out with Billy.

The Flirts finished their first song and launched into their second, a new ballad called "Wishful Thinking."

"Yes, me," Carrie replied in an even tone.

The blonde laughed. "Excuse me, but I think it's like Billy is singing right now—wishful thinking!"

Both girls cracked up. Just at that moment, though, Billy caught Carrie's eye from the stage. He winked and blew her a kiss.

Ha, Carrie thought. *I guess that shows them!* She glanced over at the girls again.

"OhmiGod, did you see that?" the brunette screeched. "Billy Sampson just blew me a kiss!"

*   *   *

"What did you think of the show tonight?" Billy asked Carrie as they walked along the beach hand in hand, their shoes in their other hands.

It was around midnight. After the Flirts' set, the whole group hung out together for a while, drinking cokes and eating pizza. Finally Billy and Carrie had begged off so they could be alone, leaving everyone else partying in the Play Café.

"It was great, as always," Carrie said lightly. "I was standing next to two die-hard Billy fans," she added.

"That's nice," Billy said with a grin. He stopped to pick up a seashell and threw it out into the water.

"One of them thought you were blowing a kiss to her instead of to me," Carrie said.

Billy threw his head back and laughed.

"It wasn't funny!" Carrie exclaimed, punching him in the arm. "They wanted to come backstage to meet you. Actually, and I quote, I think they wanted to come backstage and get 'up close and personal.'"

Billy laughed again. "Gee, and I missed out on that?"

Carrie bumped into him playfully. "You better have!"

Billy stopped walking and turned to Carrie. "That kind of stuff is real old to me these days, Carrie. You know that."

"I try to know that," Carrie said. "But . . . sometimes it's hard, you know? I watch you up onstage, and I know all these girls are fantasizing about you, wishing they could be with you—"

"You know I don't care about that stuff," Billy interrupted gently.

Carrie nodded. She stared out at the darkened ocean. "I know you don't. But sometimes I wonder, what it's going to be like when your record deal really comes through. When you're as famous as—I don't know—Pearl Jam or . . . or even Graham Perry!"

"I wish," Billy said fervently. He dropped his shoes and put his arms around Carrie. "But even if that happens, it would never change the way I feel about you."

"You don't know that," Carrie mumbled into Billy's shoulder.

"Yeah, I do," Billy insisted. He lifted her chin and gave her a soft, lingering kiss on her lips. "When you and I first got together, I wasn't looking for any big commitment," he said. "But the longer we've been together, the more I've realized how terrific you are. I wouldn't jeopardize what we have for anything. Nothing is worth it."

Carrie smiled at him, loving the way his features looked in the moonlight. "Really?"

Billy nodded. "And Carrie, I think it's time we made love with each other. Don't you?"

"Yes, I do," Carrie said softly.

Billy kissed her again, the passion escalating until she felt breathless, her knees shaky. "I didn't mean right this minute," she said when she could manage to speak.

Billy laughed. "Shall we finally make a date, milady?"

Carrie thought quickly. "Well, today's Sunday. I have tomorrow night free, because Graham and Claudia are taking

Chloe and Ian to Portland to see Elton John's show."

"Then tomorrow it is," Billy said. "I'll book us a room at the Sunset Inn, okay?"

"Um, Billy, maybe we should go somewhere else," Carrie suggested. "Like off the island?"

"Carrie, sweetheart, we have nothing to be embarrassed about," Billy said. "We're of age, we love each other—everything is fine."

"I know, you're right," Carrie said.

Billy hugged her hard. "I love you, Carrie Alden. And I'll love you forever."

"Forever is a long time," Carrie whispered.

Billy kissed her lightly. "Bet on it," he said.

FOUR

"You think we should expand?" Carrie asked doubtfully. She reached for an apple from the fruit bowl on the Hewitts' kitchen table, then put it back down again. "I don't know . . ."

It was the next afternoon, and it was pouring outside. Carrie was having a hard time concentrating on business—tonight was the big night with Billy—and everything else seemed to pale in comparison.

"My father always says you have to spend money to make money," Emma said with a shrug. "The early sales numbers on Sunset Magic look pretty good. I think we should order another two cases, and we should try to find more outlets."

Carrie ran her fingers anxiously through her hair. "I wish I knew more about this. And I wish Mr. Kane were well enough for us to ask his advice!"

"Erin says in another week or so he can have visitors," Emma said.

"Yeah, but we're not about to go in there and start talking business!"

"I don't know," Emma mused, "it might be just the thing to help him get better. You know how he is. Other than his family, perfume is the most important thing in the world to him."

"Mmmmm," Carrie said, her mind wandering. She stared out at the rain. *Today I have never slept with Billy. Tomorrow I will have slept with Billy,* she thought. *Can it possibly live up to my fantasies? Or am I going to be disappointed? And what if he's disappointed? What if—*

"Carrie? Are you okay?"

She snapped her head back to Emma. "Oh, yeah, sure," Carrie said.

"I have a feeling the fate of Sunset Magic perfume isn't the first thing on your mind right now," Emma said with a smile.

Carrie leaned her elbows on the table. "Tonight's the night, Em," she confided.

"For what?" Emma asked, looking confused. Then it dawned on her. "You and Billy? Really?"

Carrie nodded. "I'm nervous," she admitted. "I had this awful dream last night. I was standing there naked, and Billy was looking at me, and he said, 'I had no idea your thighs were that big.'"

Emma laughed and went to the refrigerator to get a pitcher of lemonade. "Oh, Carrie, you have nothing to worry about. Billy loves you. *And* you look terrific."

"Emma, Mom says I can get a Popsicle for me and one for Gina," five-year-old Katie Hewitt said, coming into the kitchen. Behind her was another little girl, with long black braids and huge eyes. Both little girls had ruffled bathing suits on. Gina even had an inflated Mickey Mouse inner tube around her waist.

"Two Popsicles coming up," Emma said, getting the frozen treats from the freezer. She handed one to each little girl.

"Thanks," Katie said. "We're going to Gina's wading pool after we eat this. Her aunt set it up in the garage so we could swim in the rain."

"Sounds like fun," Carrie said.

"It is," Katie agreed. "Mom is over there talking with Mrs. Stein, and Wills and Stinky are over there, too," Katie said quickly.

The Steins were the Hewitt's next-door neighbors. And Gina was their niece, visiting the island for a couple of weeks. Seven-year-old Wills Hewitt and the Steins' son "Stinky" were best friends who spent all their time together.

"Have fun," Emma told the kids as they scampered out of the room.

"You don't have to go watch Katie?" Carrie asked.

"No, Jane's over there. She said I could stay here." Emma looked at her watch. "I do have to do some grocery shopping, though, sometime this afternoon." She looked back over at Carrie. "I hope tonight is everything you want it to be," she said sincerely.

"What happens tonight?" Ethan Hewitt asked as he bopped into the kitchen and pulled open the fridge. Ethan was thirteen, and normally he was at Club Sunset Island during the day, where he worked as a counselor-in-training. But he'd just come from a dentist appointment and had left camp early that day.

"Aren't you supposed to let the novocaine wear off before you eat or drink anything?" Emma reminded him.

"I can't help it, I'm starving," Ethan said, reaching for a cold leg of chicken. "So, what's happening tonight?" he asked, eating the chicken and leaning against the counter.

"Nothing," Carrie said quickly.

"Oh, it's something," Ethan said. "I should have just eavesdropped. Then I would have heard the dirt."

Emma stood up. "How about if we continue this conversation up in my room?" she suggested to Carrie.

"Now, how is a guy supposed to learn about the mysteries of older women if you run up to your bedroom just when you start talking about the good stuff?" Ethan asked as Emma and Carrie ran up the stairs and into Emma's room.

"Wow, has that kid grown up!" Carrie said, plopping down on Emma's bed.

"He's grown about six inches between last summer and this summer," Emma said. "And he thinks about sex all the time."

"Me, too," Carrie agreed with a laugh. "At least it seems like it today anyway."

"So, do you have something romantic planned?" Emma asked.

"The Sunset Inn," Carrie said. "I know it's silly, but I'm really nervous!"

"It's not silly," Emma said softly. "It's a big step."

Carrie drew her knees up to her chest and wrapped her arms around them. "Did you mean what you said the other day about staying a virgin until you get married?"

"I'm thinking about it," Emma said, staring out at the rain. She looked back at Carrie. "Does it seem . . . I don't know . . . juvenile to you?"

"Not at all," Carrie assured her. "I think you should make whatever choice is right for you. I mean, what's right for

64

me might not be right for you, know what I mean?"

"I do," Emma agreed. "It's so personal. I don't feel like there's some moral high-road here—you know, like I'm somehow better or more moral if I make that choice." She got up and wandered over to the window. "All I know is that I'm glad I didn't sleep with Kurt, and I'm glad I didn't sleep with Adam . . . which doesn't mean I wasn't tempted!"

"When I leave here I have to go to the drugstore," Carrie said, "to buy condoms."

Emma turned from the window. "I remember doing that! When I thought I was going to sleep with Kurt, remember? God, it was so embarrassing! I asked for every product in the drugstore before I could bring myself to ask for the condoms! And I couldn't just pick them up because they were behind the counter!"

Carrie smacked herself in the forehead. "I can't believe what a wuss I'm being about this! I'm a grown-up! All I have to do is say 'one pack of condoms, please,' right?"

"Right," Emma said.

"Okay, I can do that. It's easy."

"Good."

Carrie stared at Emma. "This is so crazy!" she exploded. "Why can't it be like in old movies, where everything is all soft focus, and your clothes fall off, and great music plays, the couple embraces and everything fades to black."

"And in the next scene the man and the woman are both wearing something wonderful in silk," Emma said, "sharing a cigarette in bed."

"I guess back then they didn't know cigarettes could kill you," Carrie said with a sigh.

"And now we know they can, and sex can, too," Emma said. "It's so totally unromantic to be in love now!"

Carrie jumped up from the bed. "Well, I'm just going to make sure tonight is romantic, that's all there is to it. I've waited too long to mess this up. Maybe I should invest in something silky . . . nah, not my style. I guess Billy will just have to take me as I am."

"He loves you," Emma assured her,

and together they walked downstairs. "I'll walk out with you. I have to go to the store." She felt in her pocket. "Just a minute. I must have left the keys upstairs. I'll be right back."

Carrie wandered into the Hewitts' family room to wait for Emma. Just then the phone rang. After a couple of rings it stopped. *I guess Emma got it upstairs,* Carrie thought.

"Hewitt residence, this is Emma." Emma's voice echoed from the phone on the desk.

"Emma?" Carrie heard. "It's Kurt."

Someone left the speakerphone on, Carrie realized.

"Hi," Emma said, sounding surprised.

"I guess you didn't expect to hear from me," Kurt said.

I should turn it off, Carrie thought, crossing to the desk.

"No, I didn't," Emma admitted. "But . . . I'm glad to hear your voice. How are you?"

Carrie's hand hovered over the speakerphone. She knew she should press the off button, but instead she just stood there.

"Great," Kurt said. "I won a diving contest at this swim club near my cousin's house. They gave me some kind of trophy thing."

"That's nice," Emma said.

They sound like two strangers who met on an airplane, Carrie thought, still unable to bring herself to turn off the speakerphone.

"So, what's up with you?" Kurt asked.

"Not much," Emma said. "Did you get the letter I sent to you about Sunset Magic perfume?"

"Yeah," Kurt said. "I guess you and Carrie and Sam are in business now, huh?"

"We are and it's really exciting," Emma said. "We're actually starting to get reorders."

"That's nice," Kurt said.

Silence.

"So . . ." Emma finally said.

"So . . ." Kurt echoed.

More silence.

"Well, it was nice of you to call," Emma said formally.

"Yeah, sure," Kurt said. And then his

voice exploded with frustration. "Oh, hell, Emma, this is stupid. I didn't call you to make small talk. I hate it like this!"

"I hate it, too," Emma whispered.

"Dammit, Emma, I miss you. I can't stop thinking about you."

"I . . . I think about you a lot, too," Emma admitted.

"There's no one I can talk to about this!" Kurt cried. "I tried to talk it over with my cousin. He told me I was crazy. He said I should have a dart board made with your picture on it."

"A lot of your friends on the island would agree with him," Emma said.

"Well, maybe he's right," Kurt said.

"And maybe he's wrong," Emma shot back. "I've apologized to you for what I did. I can't spend my whole life apologizing!"

"I never expected you to," Kurt said stiffly.

"Besides, you made mistakes, too," Emma said. "You made me feel so pressured to get married, and you had such a hard time accepting the fact that I have money—"

"I know all about that, Emma," Kurt said.

"Do you?" Emma asked.

Kurt sighed heavily. "I'm trying to. I really am. All I know is that . . . oh, hell, I don't know anything."

"Are you . . . seeing anyone?" Emma asked in a small voice.

"No," Kurt said. "Are you?"

"No one on the island," Emma replied truthfully.

"Look, Em, I didn't call to tell you life is great, okay?" Kurt said. "I didn't call to tell you about swimming trophies or to impress you with how totally over you I am. Because I'm not. And my life stinks. Everywhere I go, I see your face."

"Oh, Kurt—"

"Sometimes I just think I'm losing my mind!" Kurt exclaimed.

"You're not, you're not," Emma assured him. "Isn't there any chance . . . I mean, maybe we need to talk in person."

"You mean I should come back to the island?" Kurt asked.

"Could you?" Emma wondered. "Even

if it were just for a visit? So that we could really talk in person?"

"I don't know . . ." Kurt began. "I was just there and it would be hard to explain to my family—"

"We have so much to say, so much that's unfinished—"

"I'm still planning on going to the Air Force Academy in the fall," he warned her.

"I don't expect you to change your plans for me," Emma said. "But I just thought if we could be together and talk . . ."

"Then what?" Kurt asked in a ragged voice.

"I don't know," Emma said. "Something."

Kurt sighed again. "I'll have to think about it. But, hey, I don't do anything else *but* think about it, who am I kidding."

"Kurt?"

"What?"

"I'm glad you called," Emma said fervently.

"Me, too," Kurt managed to say. "So long, Emma." And he hung up.

Carrie's heart was pounding in her chest when Emma came downstairs with the car keys a few minutes later.

"You won't believe who that was," Emma began.

"It was Kurt," Carrie blurted out. "Someone left the speakerphone on in here. I know I should have turned it off, but . . . I didn't."

Emma looked taken aback for a moment. "You heard everything?"

Carrie nodded guiltily. "I would make the world's worst spy," she said. "Listen, I'm really sorry . . ."

"Well, it's nice to know you're human," Emma said.

"Very," Carrie said ruefully. "He still cares about you."

Emma nodded. "I read somewhere that you never really get over your first love. I guess I'm not over him either."

"Do you think the two of you—" Carrie began.

"I don't know what to think," Emma replied. She turned the keys over in her hand. "I should have told him about Adam."

"Well, you didn't lie," Carrie pointed out.

"No, I didn't," Emma agreed. "But I certainly made it sound as if there's not anyone else in my life." Emma sighed. "Listen, this is supposed to be a really happy day for you, so don't pay attention to me. You're going to have the most romantic night of your life tonight."

"I hope!" Carrie cried.

"You are," Emma insisted. "Unlike me, you don't have to try to choose between two guys. You have the one you want. You're in love and so is he."

Carrie gave Emma a quick hug. "I really am sorry I listened in."

"It's okay," Emma said. Then she got a mischievous look on her face. "You know what this means though. The only way you can possibly pay me back is if you make those videotapes tonight that Sam asked for. She and I can watch them instead of renting a movie."

Carrie laughed. "Yeah, right."

"Oh, Billy, oh, darling!" Emma cried, imitating Carrie.

"I can't believe you!" Carrie squealed. "You sound just like Sam!"

"To know me is to love me!" Emma said, now imitating Sam, and the two of them walked out the front door and into the pouring rain.

FIVE

I can do this, Carrie told herself resolutely as she walked into Sunset Drugs a few minutes after leaving Emma's. *I'm a mature adult and I'm doing the mature thing.* She marched up to the counter and forced herself to look the pockmarked guy who worked there right in the eye.

"One package of latex condoms, please," Carrie said distinctly. She had read that latex condoms were a better barrier against disease.

"Condoms?" the guy repeated, and to Carrie's mind it sounded as if he were screaming the word.

"Yes, condoms," Carrie said, jutting her chin out slightly. *I should have gone somewhere where they're not kept behind the counter,* Carrie thought. *But why should I care? There's nothing to be embarrassed about. People buy condoms every day. I'm being smart and mature.*

A smile crossed his face. Carrie took in his name tag, which read HELLO, MY NAME IS STEVE. "Why, sure!" Steve said.

Carrie winced. *Why does his voice seem so loud? No, it's just me,* she realized. *He's being totally normal.* She told herself yet again that she had no reason to feel embarrassed or self-conscious.

"My name is Steve, by the way," the clerk added. "I've seen you in here before."

"I know your name is Steve," Carrie replied evenly.

His eyes lit up. "You asked around about me?"

"I read your name tag," Carrie said, pointing to it.

Steve laughed. "Oh, yeah, right, I forgot I was wearing it. And your name is—?"

"Look, I don't want to be rude, but I'm just here to make a purchase and leave, okay?"

"Oh, yeah, okay," Steve said.

He sounds more regretful that I don't want to get to know him than interested in my purchasing condoms, Carrie realized. *Huh. Imagine that.*

Steve handed her the box of latex condoms and she handed him some money. He smiled hopefully at her again when he gave her the change, but she just shoved it into her purse and practically ran out of the store.

"Well, that wasn't so bad, actually," Carrie murmured out loud as she got into the car. She had a great feeling of accomplishment as she started the car and headed for the Templetons.

"Why were you embarrassed?" Billy asked Carrie.

She shrugged and shook her head. "I know it was really juvenile," she told him. "I mean, people buy condoms every day. I just felt like there was a loud-speaker on, booming my request out to all of Sunset Island!"

Billy laughed and Carrie laughed with him.

It was later that evening, and the two were out on the back deck of the Sunset Inn, having a romantic dinner together. It was a magnificent evening—a few puffy cumulus clouds illuminated from below by the setting sun, the Atlantic as calm as a tabletop, and the temperature mild but not so warm as to be uncomfortable.

This is how it was meant to be, Carrie thought as she and Billy laughed together at her experience in Sunset Drugs. *The right time, the right place, the right person. I'm so glad I waited with Billy until the time was absolutely right.*

"Have I told you tonight how beautiful you look?" Billy asked Carrie, reaching for her hand.

Carrie smiled. Actually, he *had* told her about fifteen minutes before. "You know you have," Carrie said shyly, taking a sip of iced tea from the glass in front of her.

"Well, I'll tell you again, then," Billy said. "You look beautiful. Totally beautiful."

Carrie, who most of the time didn't pay

a lot of attention to clothes, had thought long and hard about what she was going to wear that night. *What do you wear when you plan to take it off in front of the guy you love?* she had asked herself. Finally, she'd selected a sheer white blouse over a camisole, and a long, full, gauzy skirt in the shades of the sunset. She'd even sprayed herself with Sunset Magic.

The waiter brought their dinners— they'd both ordered broiled fresh Atlantic salmon with rice pilaf and cucumber vinaigrette on the side—and then poured them each a glass of the sparkling cider Billy had requested as a special treat.

Billy lifted up his glass. "To you," he said.

Carrie lifted her glass. "To you," she echoed, clinking glasses with Billy.

"To ya'll!" chirped an all-too-familiar female voice from the beach down below them.

Carrie's heart sank. It was Lorell Court-land. One of Sam, Emma, and Carrie's archenemies on the island. Lorell had been keeping sort of a low profile lately, but now, apparently, she was back to her old tricks.

I'd recognize that voice anywhere, Carrie thought. *She would have to be passing by on the beach at this precise moment, wouldn't she?*

Carrie watched, slightly horrified, as Lorell bounded up the wooden steps two at a time that led from the main beach of Sunset Island up to the dining deck overlooking the ocean. She glanced at Billy, who had a look of slight bemusement on his face.

"Well," Lorell drawled, slightly out of breath, "I was just passin' by on the beach and I couldn't help but see the two of you up here, winin' and dinin' . . . You are lookin' just darling Carrie, really!"

"Thank you, Lorell," Carrie answered in a chilly tone.

Lorell looked Carrie up and down. "You know, some people think the overly full-figured can't wear skirts like that, but honestly, it doesn't look so bad on you at all!" Lorell scrutinized Carrie even closer, and little worry lines appeared between her perfectly arched eyebrows. "Of course, you are a little bosomy for a sheer white blouse—if you don't mind my telling you."

"I have a feeling that wouldn't stop you, Lorell," Carrie said, trying to maintain her composure.

"Well, Lorell," Billy began, "since this is a *private* dinner, we'll be seeing you."

"Well, of course!" Lorell exclaimed. "This is just so romantic!" She glanced down at their plates. "Identical dinners! Like two peas in a pod! That is just so cute! So, do y'all have something special planned tonight?"

"No," Carrie said quickly.

"Yes," Billy said at exactly the same time.

Lorell's eyebrows went up. "Well, well, well," she said with great insinuation. "I'd say maybe you two need to do some consultin' in private! Otherwise"—her Georgia-accented voice dropped to a whisper—"one of you might could be very, very disappointed later on. Bye-bye now!" She waved and bounded back down the steps to the beach.

Carrie groaned. "I detest her. I think she lives to make my life miserable."

"Not just yours," Billy corrected her. "Sam's, too. And Emma's. Meanwhile, we're not going to let anything spoil this night. Right?"

"Right," Carrie said gratefully, taking a bite of her salmon. It was scrumptious.

"Great fish," Billy said. "Not quite as good as my favorite restaurant back in Seattle, but still great."

"What's Seattle like?" Carrie asked, sipping her cider.

"Beautiful, really," Billy said. He got a faraway look in his eyes. "You know, I'd like to have you come back there with me sometime. To meet my family."

Carrie grinned at him, her dark eyes shining. "I'd love to."

"It's really a great city," Billy continued. "My parents live in west Seattle, which is across the Sound from downtown. There's water everywhere, and on a clear day, you can see Mount Rainier."

"I heard it rains all the time," Carrie commented.

"A lot," Billy admitted. "But on a clear

day, man, it is the most beautiful place in the world."

"Do you miss it?" Carrie asked softly.

Billy shrugged. "Some things, not others."

Carrie took another bite of her fish. "You never really talk much about your family," she commented. "I think what you told me the other day—about your older brother being in the air force and your parents not wanting you to be a musician—is the first time you've ever really opened up about them."

Billy took a sip of his cider. "When I was a kid, I wanted my dad's approval so badly."

"Every kid does," Carrie said.

"Yeah, I guess," Billy agreed. "When I was little I used to work on cars with him at his shop. I remember that as if it were yesterday. We'd take a break and go for burgers, and he'd buy me a Superman comic book."

"Sounds great," Carrie murmured.

Billy's face darkened. "Then one day I discovered music. I guess I was about ten or so. This friend of mine had a guitar, and I just fell in love with that thing. And that's when everything changed between my dad and me."

"That's so unfair," Carrie said.

"Yeah, well, I'm pretty much over thinking life is fair, you know?" Billy said, taking a bite of his fish. "I mean, if you're looking for some kind of perfect happy family like I used to see on TV when I was a kid, it wasn't us."

"That wasn't anybody," Carrie pointed out.

Billy smiled at her. "I don't know," he said, "your family comes pretty close from what I can see."

Carrie shook her head no. "Listen, no one's family is like that, including mine. We fought, we had problems, just like everyone else."

"But your parents think the world of you," Billy reminded her.

"Yeah, they do," Carrie agreed. "And I'm sure your parents think the world of you."

Billy shrugged. "No. My brother, Evan, maybe, but not me. He's the big shot in the air force, and I'm the scruffy kid with a band who's throwing his life away."

"That's not true," Carrie said fervently. "You're wonderful."

Billy reached for her hand, raised it to his lips, and kissed it. "No, babe, you're wonderful. And that's the truth."

"Oh, Billy!" Carrie said delightedly when they walked into the hotel room on the second floor of the inn. It was filled with flowers—daisies, tulips, roses— there were flowers everywhere. The tasteful antiques that decorated the room were bathed in candlelight from ten or twelve lit candles in colored safety candle-holders, so there was no chance of an accidental fire. And strewn on the white lace quilt that lay on the four-poster were hundreds of red rose petals.

"Do you like it?" Billy asked eagerly.

"I'm just . . . overwhelmed!" Carrie exclaimed breathlessly.

It's perfect, Carrie thought. *Absolutely perfect.* Billy put his arms around her and held her. She could hear his heart beating, it was so quiet. Just then she heard some loud male voices, and then some laughter, through the wall behind the bed.

"Neighbors," Billy murmured.

"I refuse to hear them," Carrie said. "Tonight there is no one alive on the entire planet except you and me."

Carrie lifted her hands to Billy's hair and felt the silky strands beneath her fingers. She raised her mouth and kissed him, lightly at first, then more passionately. His arms tightened around her waist as he kissed her back.

"Put in the other video, man!" a loud voice yelled in the next room. "Hey, who's got the brew-skis?"

I don't hear them, Carrie told herself as she kissed Billy more passionately.

Slowly she reached out and began to unbutton Billy's shirt. He dropped his hands from her waist and stood there, smiling at her. When she had his shirt unbuttoned she placed her hands, palms flat, against the hard muscles of his chest. He took her hands in his and wrapped them around him, drawing her close for another kiss.

"Gamma-gamma-pi! Gamma-gamma-pi!" male voices began to chant from the next room. The chant was followed by whistles and hoots.

"Got a dart gun?" Billy murmured. "I'd like to take some potshots at our neighbors."

"Let's put on the radio," Carrie suggested. "We can drown them out." She crossed to the clock-radio next to the bed and tuned into some classical music, which she turned up loud. "Better?"

"Much," Billy agreed. He pulled off his already unbuttoned shirt and laid it on the chair. Then he reached out for Carrie and slowly drew her over to the bed. They sat there, the scent of rose petals filling Carrie's nose, and kissed passionately.

Then slowly Billy reached for the little pearl button at the neckline of Carrie's sheer white blouse. With tantalizing slowness he unbuttoned it. Then he leaned over and softly kissed her neck. He reached for the next button. As he uncovered her skin, he kissed each spot. Finally he drew off her blouse. The candlelight played over her tanned skin, which contrasted deeply with the white of her lacy camisole.

"You are so beautiful," Billy said, and then he pulled her passionately into his arms.

Carrie fell backward on the bed, and Billy leaned over her, kissing her wildly. She wrapped her arms around his naked back, pulling him closer.

"Oh, Billy, I—"

BAM! BAM! BAM! BAM!

Carrie and Billy bolted upright. Someone was pounding on their door.

"Hotel security!" a voice yelled through the door. "Everyone outside! We're emptying the hotel! Bomb scare!"

"It's got to be a joke," Billy told Carrie. "I bet it's the yo-yos from next door!"

Then they heard the banging on the door next to them—the door that belonged to the "yo-yos," and the voice was barking the same instructions.

"I guess it's not a joke," Carrie said, looking around for her shirt.

"A bomb scare—who'd call in a bomb scare?" Billy asked. He found his shirt and pulled it on, then he quickly went around the room, blowing out the candles.

"Lorell!" Carrie said suddenly, grabbing her purse. "Or Diana!"

"Only if they knew we were here," Billy said. "We'd better move."

He reached for Carrie's hand. Just then the phone rang—Billy picked it up, and heard the hotel operator repeat the warning that the security guard had issued.

Now they moved quickly, hurrying out the door and into the hall. The hallway was filled with people in various states of undress. Carrie realized her blouse wasn't even buttoned, and she hurriedly buttoned it as she and Billy made their way toward the stairs.

"Oh, man, this is bogus!" a young guy yelled.

"We need more beer if we have to deal with this!" another yelled.

Carrie turned to see a whole group of college-age guys who clearly had been in the room next to her and Billy. Just as she was fumbling with the buttons on her blouse, a pair of eyes met hers.

Blue eyes, in a skinny, pockmarked face.

Steve. The guy from Sunset Drugs. With his fraternity buddies.

Carrie froze in embarrassment. Steve looked from her to Billy, then back at her again. "Hubba hubba!" he bellowed. His frat buddies cracked up, falling all over each other. He turned drunkenly to Billy. "Hey, man, you are one lucky guy—"

The next thing Carrie knew, Billy was standing in Steve's face. He grabbed Steve's T-shirt and practically lifted him from the floor. "Listen buddy," Billy said, "there's a bomb scare on. If I were you, right about now I'd be—"

"Leaving!" Steve replied jauntily. "C'mon guys, we're outta here." He and his frat buddies ran down the hallway to the stairs, still guffawing and laughing.

"We're outta here, too," Billy said, putting his arm around Carrie.

"I cannot believe that just happened," Carrie said as the two of them traipsed down the stairs. "That was—"

"The guy from the drugstore," Billy finished for her, as they hurried through the lobby and out into the night with all the other hotel guests and personnel. "I recognized him. He's basically harmless."

Carrie shivered in the night air. Billy wrapped his arm around her. "A bomb scare? This is just unbelievable!"

Billy chuckled. "No kidding. This gives new meaning to the term 'delayed gratification'!"

"What a night," Carrie commented dispiritedly, leaning her head against Billy's shoulder.

"We'll get another chance," Billy promised her.

I hope so, Carrie thought. *And I hope it's soon. Because the way things have gone today, I can't take many more first times like this!*

SIX

"Sam should be here any minute," Emma said to Carrie the next morning as the two friends were sitting together in the Hewitts' kitchen, Emma drinking tea, Carrie sipping a cup of coffee. Jeff, Jane and the kids were in Portland for the morning, so Emma had a few hours off to relax.

Carrie looked at her watch. "I can't stay very long," she said. "I have to take the kids to the country club."

Emma had invited both Sam and Carrie to stop by for a while. She'd told them she had something she wanted to talk over with them. Carrie had arrived on time, and Sam—despite her telling Carrie that she had turned over a new leaf—was late, as usual.

"You want a piece of this banana bread?" Emma asked Carrie as she cut herself a thin slice. "Katie and I baked it yesterday."

"You're so domestic," Carrie teased.

"Well, before I had this job I had never cooked a thing in my life," Emma admitted. "When I was a kid, either I was at boarding school or I was home, where servants did everything. And then once I got to college, I ate out all the time."

"Rough life," Carrie said with a chuckle.

"Well, anyway," Emma said, taking a bite of the bread, "I found out I like to cook."

Carrie sipped her coffee. "You're deliberately not asking me about last night, aren't you?"

Emma's eyes widened. "No, really—"

"Yes, really," Carrie said. "You are such a well-bred person, Emma."

Emma wrinkled her nose. "That doesn't sound like a compliment."

"Well, I meant it as one," Carrie said.

Emma blew on her tea to cool it off. "Okay, I admit, I'm curious. But I also think it's private, between you and Billy." She put down her teacup. "Just tell me this, are you happy?"

"No!" Carrie cried, though she laughed as she said it.

Emma looked alarmed. "You mean it wasn't wonderful?"

Just then the front door opened, and Sam came barreling in. Carrie smiled— the outfit she had on was so . . . so Sam. It featured a child's ruby velvet babydoll dress—from some thrift store, no doubt—with the arms cut off. The dress reached the top of Sam's thighs. Under that she wore tiny cutoffs with red peace symbols hand-painted all over them, and her red cowboy boots.

Carrie looked over at Emma, who had on a plain white T-shirt and white cotton shorts, in which she managed to look perfect. Then she looked down at her own baggy overalls over a red tank top, and thought for the zillionth time how totally different the three of them were.

"Okay, I'm late, I'm sorry. Now tell me every detail of everything you did last night," she demanded from Carrie. She pulled out a chair, plopped down, and peered into Carrie's face.

"Sam, chill out," Emma told her.

"Please," Sam snorted. "Tell me you aren't dying to hear about it."

"Well, I'm interested," Emma allowed. She thought for a moment. "Okay, I'm dying to hear about it," she admitted.

Carrie sighed. "The truth is," she said, "there isn't anything to tell."

"Wow," Sam breathed. "That bad, huh? Man, you can't tell by looking at a guy, huh? I mean, to look at Billy, you'd think he'd be this studly hunk—"

"Uh, Sam," Carrie interrupted, "you are jumping to the wrong conclusion. What actually happened is . . . we didn't do it."

"What!" Sam cried. "After all that buildup? What happened?"

Carrie related the whole story, including the part about Steve and his frat brothers. By the time she finished, all three girls were shaking with laughter.

"Oh, my God!" Sam squealed. "That's the funniest story I ever heard in my life!"

"Well, it wasn't funny last night," Carrie managed to gasp, though at the moment she was laughing her head off about it.

"A bomb scare!" Emma cried, wiping the tears of laughter from her eyes. "I can't believe it!"

Carrie broke into a fresh burst of laughter. "Anyway, the hotel never did blow up. But they wouldn't let us back inside for hours. Finally we just went home."

"You must be so disappointed," Emma commiserated. "I'm really sorry."

"I am," Carrie admitted. "And it was so perfect, so romantic—"

"You'll get over it," Sam said quickly. "The big thing is, now when are you and Billy going to finally do the deed?"

Carrie shrugged. "I don't know," she said. "Graham and Claudia are leaving tomorrow night to go to New York for a few days. And it can't be tonight because Billy has to be in Portland. Besides, I'm supposed to stay with the kids."

"Why don't you just commandeer Graham and Claudia's bedroom while they're out of town?" Sam asked, reaching for a piece of banana bread.

"Gee, that sounds like a great way to lose my job," Carrie replied.

"I was kidding," Sam said, her mouth full. "Well, sort of."

Carrie looked at her watch again. "I have to leave in a few minutes—although I'd much rather stay here than spend the afternoon playing Chutes and Ladders with Chloe."

"I used to love that game," Sam said, reaching for another slice of banana bread. "So, Emma-bo-Bemma, now that we've heard Carrie's non-news, why'd you invite us over?"

Emma picked up a large yellow envelope and held it up. "This."

"What? Is it from Kurt?" Sam asked.

"It's Adam's screenplay," Emma explained.

Carrie remembered what Emma had said Adam had told her about the screenplay: that it was the most important thing in the world to him, that it was the culmination of his life's work to that point, and that it was as if he had put his whole heart down on paper for the world to see. She searched Emma's face for a clue as to what she thought. She couldn't read a thing.

"So," Sam said nonchalantly, reaching for Carrie's coffee, "is the movie going to be a smash hit and is there a part in it for me?"

Emma sighed. "I don't know what to tell you about it."

"What's it called?" Carrie asked.

Emma took the screenplay out of the envelope and showed it to her two friends. It was about a hundred and thirty pages, and the title page read:

FRANK AND STEIN

An Original Screenplay

by Adam Briarly

"*Frank and Stein?*" Sam asked, a quizzical look on her face.

"Funny title," Carrie offered.

"It's an updated version of the Frankenstein story," Emma explained.

"You mean a mad scientist creates a creature, and the creature gets loose?" Sam asked.

"Something like that," Emma said, nodding. "In this version the scientist is named Stein, the creature is named Frank, and the whole thing takes place in Washington, D.C."

"It sounds really funny!"

"That's the problem," Emma said. "It's not supposed to be funny. It's supposed to be serious."

"Are you sure?" Sam asked. "Maybe he meant the whole thing, as, like, a spoof. You know, like they do on *In Living Color* or on *Saturday Night Live*."

Emma shook her head no. "There's this letter from Adam with the screenplay, telling me how dramatic it all is. He didn't mean it to be funny. Here, take a look at this." She opened the screenplay to page eighty-four, a page she had already marked with a yellow Post-it note.

Sam and Carrie leaned over and looked

at the page. From top to bottom, margin to margin, it was one long speech, delivered by the monster Frank, and the direction at the top instructed that Frank was to deliver this monologue directly to the camera.

"To the camera?" Sam asked, looking puzzled.

Emma nodded.

"It's not dialogue?" Carrie asked.

"It's a monologue," Emma surmised. "And there are about fifteen just like it at various places in the movie."

"In theater that's called breaking the fourth wall," Carrie offered.

"What does that mean?" Emma asked.

"We studied it in my American Theater class last semester at Yale," Carrie said. "Usually there is an imaginary wall between the actor and the audience. Like when an actor looks out at the audience, the audience doesn't exist. Instead, it's the inside of his house, or the night sky, whatever."

"So, can you break the fourth wall in a movie?" Sam asked, looking dubious.

"It's been done," Carrie acknowledged. She leaned over and looked at the endless monologue again. "But I don't think it's ever been done for *this* long."

"Sounds boring," Sam quipped. "Sorry, bro."

"Well, maybe he just needs to do some rewrites," Carrie suggested.

"A whole lot of rewrites," Sam added.

"So, what do I do now?" Emma asked.

"What do you mean?" Sam asked, reaching for another slice of banana bread. "This bread is de-lish, by the way."

"Adam asked me to call him and tell him what I think," Emma explained. "This means so much to him. What am I supposed to say?"

Carrie and Sam looked at each other.

"I think," Carrie said slowly, "if he asked you, he really wants to know your opinion."

"I guess," Emma said doubtfully. "But what if I'm wrong? I'm not qualified to critique a screenplay!"

"Look, I bet the most famous writers in the world weren't great on the first draft of their very first screenplay," Carrie pointed out.

"I guess that's true, too," Emma agreed. "And I know how much this means to him. . . ."

"So are you going to call him?" Sam asked, licking a crumb off her finger.

Emma thought a moment. "Absolutely," she said. "And I'm going to be really encouraging, too. You're right, Carrie. This is probably just an early draft. And the most talented writers in the world were once neophytes. . . . "

"What's that?" Sam asked.

"Beginners," Emma explained.

"Why didn't you just say so, then?" Sam said with dignity.

"I won't lie," Emma decided. "I won't say it's perfect and wonderful. But I'll be totally supportive and upbeat. I can do that!"

"So, cool," Sam commented. "You're doing the right thing. Only if I were you, I'd hope for one thing."

"What's that?" Emma asked.

"That Adam isn't home, and that his answering machine is on!"

Three hours later, Carrie was at the Templetons' house, playing Chutes and Ladders with Chloe Templeton, when the doorbell rang.

Billy, Carrie thought. *He told me he'd try to stop by this afternoon.*

Carrie and Chloe got up from their game together to go answer the door.

"Billy!" Chloe squealed, lifting her arms to him.

"How are my two favorite girls?" Billy asked. He leaned over and scooped Chloe up into his arms, and the little girl laughed with delight.

"Play airplane!" she cried, indicating that Billy should swing her around above his head.

"If I play airplane with you, will you go watch videos for a few minutes so I can talk to Carrie?" Billy asked.

"Sure!" Chloe promised. "Make me go really high!"

True to his word, Billy took Chloe into the yard and swung her around like an airplane for a few minutes. When the little girl had enough, he set her down, and she obediently went back into the living room and switched on MTV on the big video monitor.

"Chloe, how about a different show?" Carrie suggested.

"I like MTV," Chloe said stubbornly, holding tightly to the remote control.

Carrie glanced at the screen. Images of writhing girls wearing leather bikinis filled the screen. She sighed and went back out to Billy.

"I'm telling you, man," Ian was saying to Billy, "girls just aren't worth it."

"Yeah, it can be tough," Billy commiserated.

"I mean, one minute they love you, the next minute they won't give you the time of day!" Ian said. "It's got to be hormonal or something!"

Carrie walked over to the guys and Ian gave her a dirty look.

"What did I do?" Carrie asked him.

"You're female, that's enough," Ian said with disgust, and he stomped off.

"What's up with him?" Billy asked Carrie.

"I think Becky is giving him a hard time," Carrie explained. "She's seeing some other guy."

"Ouch," Billy said. He and Carrie sat out on the porch. Billy put his arm around Carrie's shoulders and kissed her cheek gently.

"I have to get back to the kids soon," she warned him. "Claudia and Graham are upstairs."

"So I guess that means I can't throw you down on the porch and ravage you, huh?"

"Well, you could," Carrie allowed. "It wouldn't be any worse than what Chloe is watching on MTV right now."

Billy laughed and hugged her tight. "That was quite the adventure last night, huh?"

"Quite," Carrie murmured into his neck.

"Next time," Billy said, "don't go calling in any bomb scares to the Inn."

"A bomb scare, who would have believed it?" Carrie asked, shaking her head ruefully.

"They caught the guy, by the way,"

Billy told her. "It was some cook who had just gotten fired. I heard it on the news. And there wasn't a bomb either. The guy planted a suitcase full of electric clocks down in the boiler room just to scare the hell out of everyone."

"It worked," Carrie said with a laugh.

"Anyway," Billy said, nuzzling Carrie's hair, "next time will be *the* time. I keep dreaming about you . . . about all of you."

"Sam said I should commandeer Graham's bedroom," Carrie reported as she rested her head on Billy's shoulder.

"Oh, great," Billy said, chuckling. "Why do I think Graham and Claudia wouldn't be so thrilled with that concept?"

"What concept won't we be thrilled with?" Claudia asked, coming out on to the porch.

Carrie blushed. *I hope she didn't hear what we were talking about,* she thought to herself. "The concept of . . . Chloe watching MTV," Carrie invented quickly.

Claudia shrugged. "You try to stop her. Carrie, I need you to run over to the dry cleaners and pick up the clothes you left there day before last. Here's the ticket." She handed the pink slip of paper to Carrie.

"Sure," Carrie said. "Billy was just leaving anyway."

"Oh, he can go with you, I don't care," Claudia said. "But I need you to make dinner for the kids when you get back." She went back into the house.

"I'm just a working girl," Carrie quipped, slipping the dry-cleaning ticket into the pocket of her jeans.

"I have to go," Billy said. He hugged her close. "So, when do we get to spend the night together?"

"Claudia and Graham are leaving tomorrow," Carrie reminded him, leaning against his chest. "And then I'm on duty with the kids full-time."

"What about tomorrow afternoon?" Billy asked. "Pres is working at Wheels, Jay and Jake are in some kind of bike rally. No one will be home at my house."

"I don't know," Carrie said. "In the afternoon? And what if someone changes their plans and shows up?"

"I have my own room with an actual

lock on the door," Billy said. "And last time I checked, couples were allowed to be together in the afternoon."

"I'll think about it," Carrie promised.

"You do that," Billy said, kissing her lightly. "And I'll be thinking about you."

SEVEN

"What did Emma say again?" Carrie asked.

"She said she had to see us. She said it was about Adam, and she sounded really upset," Sam relayed.

It was the next day, and Carrie had gotten a phone call from Sam saying that Emma had called her, and that she wanted both Carrie and Sam to meet her out at the far dunes at noon. Neither Sam nor Carrie had been able to get a car, so Sam had called Pres, who was driving them to the dunes in the band's van.

"What could Adam have said to her that upset her so much?" Carrie mused, leaning forward in the van so she could hear Sam better.

"Got me," Sam replied. "Wait, unless he called her last night and said he's in love with someone else or something. I mean, it couldn't be about the screenplay. She said she was going to tell him how great it was."

"Well, she said she was going to encourage him anyway," Carrie clarified. She looked quickly at her watch. She couldn't completely keep her mind on Emma and Adam. Billy had called her that morning and reissued his invitation. No one would be home at the Flirts' house all day. And Carrie didn't have to be back at the Templetons until six o'clock, when the limousine was coming to pick up Graham and Claudia to take them to the airport.

I told him I didn't know if I'd come over or not, Carrie recalled. *I don't know why I didn't just jump at the chance. No, wait, I do know why. Because somehow making love at the Flirts' house in the afternoon, and not being able to sleep in Billy's arms afterward, is not the way I imagined all this would unfold!*

"Maybe Adam wants to come visit the island," Carrie guessed, trying to keep her mind on something other than Billy.

"Nah," Sam said. "He always wants to visit her. It's gotta be more than that."

"It can't be too bizarre," Carrie said. "Adam is a great guy."

"*Guy* is the operative word there, even if he is my brother," Sam said with a shrug. "Guys do bizarre things."

"Watch it now," Pres drawled, a slight smile on his face.

Sam leaned over and kissed Pres' cheek. "You're a prince in guy-dom," she decreed.

Pres pulled the van into a small parking lot, then he turned to Sam. "I hate to put you on a time frame here, but I have to work at Wheels this afternoon, which means I have to skedaddle from here in around forty-five minutes."

"We'll watch the time," Carrie promised, looking at her watch. She and Sam scrambled out of the van.

Pres picked up the novel he was reading, something called *She's Come Undone,* and settled back to wait.

"Hey, why don't you come and at least say hello to Emma," Sam suggested, sticking her head back in the van's window. "You always cheer her up."

"Okay," Pres agreed. He got out of the van and the three of them climbed the first dune, and then spied Emma, sitting by herself on an old blanket.

"Well, she sure looks like a lonely pup," Pres murmured as they climbed through the sand to reach Emma.

"Hi," Carrie said, dropping down on the blanket next to her friend.

Emma attempted a small smile. "Hi," she said softly.

"Look, I can't stand this," Sam said, plopping down next to Carrie. "If anyone died or anything truly awful, just blurt it out and get it over with."

"I just came to say hey," Pres said, kneeling down next to Emma and putting his hand on her hair.

Emma took his hand in hers. "Stay," she asked him.

"Well, it doesn't seem really right—" Pres protested.

"No, I really want you to," Emma said, staring into his eyes. "Maybe a guy's point of view would help me."

Pres shrugged and settled down on the sand, waiting.

Emma took a deep breath. "You know I tried to call Adam about this screenplay while you guys were over. And he wasn't home."

"Cut to the chase," Sam said impatiently, brushing some windblown hair out of her eyes.

"I finally reached him last night about ten," Emma continued. "And of course he wanted to know what I thought of *Frank and Stein.*"

"A screenplay he wrote," Sam filled in for Pres.

"Well, I did what I told you guys I was going to do," Emma said. "I was as encouraging as I could be without actually lying. And it was difficult—I mean, what do I know about screenplays? Maybe it's wonderful and I'm just not knowledgeable enough to see it!"

"And maybe it sucks the big one," Sam said with a shrug.

"All those monologues to the camera," Carrie said, shaking her head ruefully. "It seems kind of pretentious."

"But I didn't want to say that," Emma explained.

"Criticizing someone's art can be dangerous," Pres pointed out.

Carrie nodded in agreement. "Because it feels personal. When someone rejects my photos, I feel as if they're rejecting me."

"That's just it," Emma said earnestly. "I didn't want him to feel rejected, and I don't feel qualified to judge his screenplay. I know how much it means to him—"

"So, what did you finally say?" Sam asked.

"I said I thought it had a lot of potential," Emma related.

"Potential—ouch—" Pres winced. "That's the artistic kiss of death."

"He didn't take it that way," Emma said. "I told him that I thought his passion for the subject matter really came through. I tried to be encouraging. . . ."

"That was nice of you," Carrie said.

Emma shook her head and looked bewildered. "Maybe it was stupid of me, I don't know. He kept saying 'really? really?' sort of begging me to say more good things. And so . . . so I did. Maybe I got carried away, but he sounded so hopeful, so happy—"

"You were trying to be nice," Carrie said, "that's all. You wanted him to feel good. There's no harm in that."

"Well, I guess it worked—better than I ever imagined," Emma said ironically. "Adam seemed to feel great. And then he said, 'Emma, you understand what art really is, the big Hollywood studios don't. Which is why I want you to finance my movie.'"

Carrie's jaw dropped open. "He said *what*?"

"He asked me to finance *Frank and Stein*," Emma repeated wearily. "He wants me to put up the money. He said he can do it on one and a half million."

"Dang," Pres said under his breath. "Dumb move."

"Why is it so dumb?" Sam asked, sounding defensive.

"How can you even ask that?" Carrie wondered.

"Hold on, let's not get all huffy," Sam said. "I mean, Adam believes it's a good script. And now he believes that his friend believes it's a good script, too. So why shouldn't he go to his friend to finance it if she can afford it, which she can?"

"But I thought I was supposed to be reading it as a friend, not as a financier!" Emma exclaimed.

"That's true," Sam agreed. "But I really, truly don't see what the big deal is! Why is what Adam did so terrible?"

"Because it's a sure way to ruin their romance," Pres told Sam with exasperation. "Surely you can see that!"

"No, I can't actually," Sam said evenly, folding her arms.

"I'm sorry, Sam," Emma said, "I know Adam is your brother, and you know I care about him, but I can't believe he did this either!"

"Why not?" Sam asked, her chin jutting out.

"Because I feel like he's using me!" Emma cried.

"This boy ain't worthy of you, Em," Pres said gruffly. "Cut the fool loose."

"Why, so you can have her?" Sam shot at Pres.

For a moment, no one said anything. The silence was deafening.

Carrie shut her eyes. *Sam is so insecure about Pres,* she thought. *Even if Emma and Pres were attracted to each other, they'd never act on it.* She opened her eyes.

"I'm sure Sam didn't mean that," Carrie finally said.

Sam refused to speak.

Pres sighed. "Emma is my friend, Sam."

"I know that," Sam said, struggling with herself.

"And you're the one who suggested I get out of the van and come try to help," Pres added.

"I know that, too," Sam said.

"Look, this is my fault," Emma said quickly. "I didn't mean to drag everyone into this." She looked over at Sam. "And

119

I should have known it would be hard for you since Adam is your brother."

Sam took a deep breath. "Maybe I am being influenced by that, but maybe I just feel how I feel." She picked up a handful of sand and let it fall through her fingers. "You can't pretend you're not rich, Emma. And you shouldn't be so surprised if someone in your life wants you to use your money to help them out." She looked Emma in the eye. "Look what you did for Erin's father. You invested in a perfume, for God's sake! And Adam is a lot closer to you than Mr. Kane!"

"The difference," Emma said, "is that Mr. Kane never asked me for anything. I decided I wanted to start a perfume business. I went to him."

"Oh, so you have to have all the control as well as all the money," Sam said coldly.

"As long as it's my money, yes," Emma replied in a steely voice. She and Sam stared at each other for a moment.

"Why are the two of you fighting?" Carrie demanded.

"I'm outta here," Pres said. "I'll meet

ya'll back at the van." He got up and walked away.

"Not a very smart move, Sam," Emma said. "You just got Pres back. It's not a very good time to push him away."

"I don't need guy advice from you!" Sam said. "You don't seem to have that part of your own life too under control at the moment!"

"Stop it!" Carrie said, pounding her fist into the sand. "God, this is horrible! We're best friends! What are you two doing?"

Sam looked after Pres, who was now a tiny dot in the distance. "I messed up," she said in a low voice.

"Pres will forgive you," Emma said with a sigh.

Sam looked at her. "And you?"

"I don't want to fight with you, Sam," Emma said.

Sam dug her toes into the sand. "You've never not had money, Em," she tried to explain. "You have no idea what that's like. I mean, if you were Adam, and your dream was to make a movie, you could just go ahead and finance your own dream. But most people can't do that."

"I know," Emma said softly.

"But you don't know what it *feels* like," Sam said sadly.

"I still think it was wrong for Adam to ask me," Emma said. "Now I wonder if that's what was in his mind all along. Did he always just like me because he thought I could finance a movie for him? How long has he been planning this?"

"I don't believe it ever had anything to do with money," Carrie said.

"Well, we'll never know for sure, will we?" Emma asked. She brushed some sand off her knee. "If I say no—and I have to say no because I don't think the screenplay is very good—then what happens to our relationship?"

No one had an answer.

Emma looked at Sam. "You're right, Sam, I can afford to do it. I would hardly even miss the money. And Adam knows that. But once I say no to him, once I crush his dream, how do you think he's going to feel about me?"

There was no sound but the call of one

lonesome gull circling in the clear blue sky.

"You came," Billy said happily when he opened his front door a half hour later and saw Carrie standing there.

"Pres dropped me off," Carrie said.

Billy opened the door and Carrie walked into the shabby living room of the Flirts' house. "Pres?" he wondered.

"He drove Sam and me out to the dunes to meet Emma," Carrie explained, taking a seat on the couch. Quickly she told Billy the whole story.

"Whoa," Billy commented, putting his arm around Carrie on the couch.

"It was terrible to hear Sam and Emma fighting. Sam was wrong, but I could see her point, too."

Billy held her close. "Relationships can be hard, huh?"

Carrie nodded into Billy's chest. "I'm so glad ours isn't."

Billy lifted Carrie's face and kissed her lightly on the lips. "How would you like a back rub?"

Carrie laughed. "That's what boys used

to say in high school when they wanted to try to feel a girl up."

"Well, I do want to feel you up," Billy said, trying to keep a straight face.

"I want to feel you up, too," Carrie joked, "but at the moment I just want some peace and quiet."

"I can arrange that," Billy said softly. He stood up and reached out for Carrie. She took his hand. Slowly he led her into his bedroom. A patchwork quilt thrown over the bed was covered in rose petals.

"Oh, Billy," Carrie said, throwing her arms around him. "You didn't even know if I'd come over!"

"What can I tell you?" he said lightly, inhaling the rich scent of her hair. "I believe in positive thinking."

"I love you so much," Carrie said fervently. She wrapped her arms around his neck and kissed him, softly at first, then harder, exploring his mouth with hers. She looked back over at the bed, at the shabby, mismatched furniture that decorated the room. "I thought it wouldn't be romantic to be here with you like this," she said. "But I was wrong. Totally wrong."

She took Billy's hand and led him over to the bed. Then she lay down on top of the rose petals and held out her arms.

He came to her.

And then they weren't in his bedroom, in his house, or even on Sunset Island.

Carrie and Billy were totally in a world of their own.

EIGHT

Billy. Billy. Billy.

It was eight o'clock that evening, and Carrie lay on the couch in the Templetons' living room, staring up at the ceiling, reliving over and over again the wonderful, beautiful, amazing experience she had had that afternoon with the guy she loved.

Fortunately Chloe had gone to bed early, and Ian was down in the basement, writing a song for his band, Lord Whitehead and the Zit People. *Which means I have nothing more important to do than to think about the feel of Billy's lips on mine,* Carrie thought dreamily, *the feel of his strong arms wrapped around me . . .*

The phone rang on the table next to the couch, and Carrie languidly reached over to pick it up.

"Hi, there," she said, still caught up in her memories of the afternoon.

"Carrie?" came Sam's voice. "If I didn't know that you don't do drugs, I'd say that you sound seriously one toke over the line."

"I'm just . . . happy," Carrie said with a contented sigh.

"Well, good, that makes one of us," Sam said. "I feel like dog meat about what happened this afternoon with Emma. I can't believe I said some of the stuff I said. So I want to apologize."

"You don't have to apologize to me," Carrie said, reaching for one of the grapes in the bowl of fruit at her side and popping it into her mouth. "You have to apologize—"

"I know," Sam cut her off, "to Emma and to Pres. I already did to Pres. He's okay about it. At least he says he is."

"That's good."

"I really stuck the old foot in the mouth with him, huh?"

"Yep," Carrie agreed.

"I don't know why I get so insecure sometimes," Sam said with a sigh. "Sometimes I secretly feel like Pres and Emma are perfect for each other. But I'm being dumb, right?"

"Right," Carrie agreed firmly.

"That's what Pres said, too. He said everyone's allowed to be insecure every six months or so."

"He's a great guy," Carrie said.

"Yeah," Sam agreed.

"So, did you call Emma?" Carrie asked her. "It was so awful, listening to the two of you fighting!"

"I just called her," Sam replied.

"And?"

"I apologized," Sam reported. "Sort of anyway."

"What does that mean?" Carrie asked her, reaching for another grape.

"I told her I was sorry I went off on her—"

"Are you?" Carrie asked.

"Yeah," Sam said. "But—"

"But what?"

"But I'm not sorry for my opinion,"

Sam said a little huffily. "I still think I'm right. Who else is Adam going to ask to finance his movie besides people he thinks might do it and not rip him off? I mean, the way I see it . . ."

Carrie's mind started to wander. She saw Billy's face right before she'd left his house, gazing down at her with such love and tenderness.

He held me at the front door, she remembered, *and he told me I was the most important thing in the world to him, more important even than his music. Then he kissed me so softly, and he said he loved me, and then . . .*

"Yo, Carrie!" Sam's voice bellowed through the phone. "Are you still here?"

"Oh, yeah, sure," Carrie said, guiltily snapping back to the conversation.

"So, what do you think?" Sam demanded.

I've got to admit that at the moment, Carrie thought, *I'm not worrying very much about Adam and his screenplay and whether Emma puts money into it or not. This isn't very fair to Sam. She's pretty upset about this, and I'm not giving her my attention. I'd better tell her.*

"Listen, Sam," Carrie said, "can we talk about this another time? Maybe even later tonight?"

"Well, okay," Sam replied, though Carrie detected a hurt tone in her voice. "You probably agree with Emma anyway—"

"It's not that," Carrie interjected. "I'm just . . . thinking about other things."

"What other things?" Sam queried.

"Billy," Carrie answered quietly. "Billy Sampson. Billy James Sampson. Did you know his middle name is James?"

"Gee, no," Sam said dryly. "Let me get right over to the *Breakers* and offer Kristy the story for the front page."

"It's a beautiful name, though, isn't it?" Carrie said.

"Uh, Carrie? Babe? No offense, but you sound like one of the zombies in *Invasion of the Body Snatchers*," Sam told her.

"Uh-huh," Carrie said, a silly grin on her face.

"Yowza, if even contemplating doing the wild thing with Billy makes you this crazy, I'm scared to think how you're gonna act after you finally go through with it!" Sam exclaimed.

"That's just it," Carrie said, her voice dropping low.

"Just what?"

"We finally did it," Carrie said. "We made love. This afternoon, at the Flirts' house."

Silence.

"I can't believe it," Carrie remarked lightly. "I have finally found a way to leave you speechless."

"Girlfriend!" Sam finally cried. "You did it? You actually did it?"

"Yes," Carrie said quietly. "We did."

"Nu?"

"Nu?" Carrie asked. Then she remembered this was one of those Yiddish expressions Sam had learned from her birth parents. "Oh, you're asking me what it was like?"

"Carrie Alden, for a girl who's going to be a sophomore at Yale, sometimes you are a little slow on the uptake," Sam told her.

"It was wonderful," Carrie said simply. "Totally, completely wonderful."

"I don't want to hear 'wonderful,'" Sam groused. "I need details! Wait, I'll get a pen—"

"Nope," Carrie replied.

"One detail."

"Nope."

"Pretty please?" Sam asked, doing an absolutely perfect imitation of Chloe Templeton, which cracked Carrie up completely.

"Okay, okay!" Carrie relented. She waited a moment. "Billy covered his bed with rose petals."

"Get out of town!" Sam exclaimed.

"He really did," Carrie assured her.

"Unbelievable," Sam marveled. "That's twice! It's like out of a book or something. Okay, so there were these rose petals. Did you undress yourself or did he undress you?"

"Sam—"

"Were you like, self-conscious when he saw you naked? Did you keep the lights on? What did Billy look like? Did you feel like you had to suck your stomach in all the time—"

"Sam, you can ask anything you want,

but you're not getting any answers," Carrie said mildly.

"How can you do this to me?" Sam wailed. "Who can I ask if I can't ask you?"

"You'll have to wait until you're ready and find out for yourself," Carrie said.

"Please," Sam snorted, "you know I'm going to be a virgin until I'm so old, no one will want me!"

"I'll tell you this," Carrie said, her voice serious. "I'm very, very glad Billy and I waited until we'd been together this long, until we both felt totally certain that we want to spend our lives together—"

"No, don't tell me you're getting married!" Sam yelled.

"We're not," Carrie said, a smile in her voice. "Not yet anyway. This afternoon was the most romantic, beautiful experience of my life, and I don't think it could have been nearly as perfect if I'd rushed into it—"

"Hold up," Sam interrupted. "You guys did use a condom, right? I mean, it wasn't so romantic that you didn't stop to—"

"We used one," Carrie assured her. "I

might have been in a state of bliss, but I didn't get stupid all of a sudden."

"I don't know," Sam said, "I've heard love can make the old I.Q. slump big-time."

"Not mine," Carrie said. She reached for another grape.

"Well, I suppose I don't blame you for not telling me the down-and-dirty details," Sam said grudgingly. "However, if you change your mind, call me any time, day or night."

"I'll keep that in mind," Carrie said with a laugh.

"I guess I can see why you don't want to talk about my petty problems tonight," Sam said. "Anyway, I gotta go—I haven't even cleaned up from dinner yet, and Dan is bringing Kiki—that actress he's dating—over here to watch a video."

"You can call me later if you want," Carrie said. "I promise to concentrate."

"Forget it," Sam said, "you're hopeless for at least twenty-four hours." She was quiet for a moment. "Car?"

"Hmmmmm?"

"I'm really happy for you," Sam said warmly.

Carrie heard the beep-beep sound that meant that someone was trying to get through on call waiting. She and Sam said a quick good-bye, and then Carrie turned her attention to the incoming call.

"Templeton residence," Carrie said, this time remembering to sound professional. "Carrie Alden speaking."

"Carrie?" a male voice said to her. "It's Adam."

Adam. Carrie drew in a quick breath. *Now, why would he be calling me? I didn't even know he had my number.* Carrie had no idea whether Adam knew that she knew anything at all about his screenplay, and that Adam had asked Emma to finance his film, so she decided to play it very cautiously.

"Adam!" Carrie said. "What a surprise! How are you?"

"I'm calling about Emma," Adam said, his voice a little hyper-sounding. "Do you know that I sent her a screenplay called *Frank and Stein?*"

"Well, yes," Carrie said slowly, feeling

her way through the conversation. "Emma mentioned something to me about it."

"Good!" Adam said quickly. "Then you're familiar with the project."

"A little," Carrie admitted.

"It's going to win at the Sundance Festival someday—" Adam promised.

"Sundance?" Carrie echoed.

"A very important film festival that Robert Redford started," Adam explained. "I've always dreamed of having a film that I wrote and directed entered at Sundance."

"Well, that's good—" Carrie replied.

"But I've got to get it financed!" Adam interrupted her. "You don't know what it's like in Hollywood! It's cutthroat. Every person you meet on the street has written a screenplay. I mean, people would kill—literally kill—in this town to get a deal with a studio."

"I'm sure that's true—" Carrie began.

"I can't even get a decent agent to take me on," Adam continued. "And without an agent, forget it. I've got friends from my class at U.C.L.A. who are already with the big agencies! Well, I don't write commercial crap! Which is why I have to find independent financing!"

A thought sprung into Carrie's mind—Emma telling her that it sounded like maybe Adam was doing speed, he seemed so manic. *Could that be it?* Carrie wondered. *But he seemed way too smart to do anything that dumb.*

"Adam," Carrie finally said gently, "I only work for Graham Templeton, I don't have any money—"

Adam interrupted Carrie again. "Listen, Carrie," he said, "there's no need to pretend with me. I know you and Emma and Sam talk about everything. Did Emma tell you that I called her about maybe financing my picture?"

"Yes," she admitted.

"So you know she hasn't told me one way or the other yet," Adam related.

Oh, God, Carrie realized. *That's right. Emma hasn't told him no yet, even though that's what she's going to say, and I know it.*

"She told me she had to think about it," Carrie hedged.

"I can understand that," Adam said.

"It's a big project. But I know how close the two of you are. And I know you're an artist, like me, so you can understand. You can convince her!"

He wants me to convince Emma? I can't believe this! Carrie thought.

"Um, Adam, did you think about asking Sam?" Carrie queried.

"I thought about it," Adam admitted, "but it wouldn't work. Emma would just think that it's because Sam's my sister. Half sister anyway."

"Adam, I can't get in the middle of this," Carrie said gently.

"Look, Carrie, I'm baring my soul to you, okay?" Adam said, his voice intense-sounding. "Believe me, I wouldn't be making this phone call if I thought I had a choice. Do you know what it's like to have a dream and to watch it slip away? Do you?"

"Adam," Carrie said finally, "this is something that you're going to have to work out with Emma. I haven't even read your script!"

"I'll send it to you," Adam offered

quickly. "Overnight. You'll have it by ten-thirty tomorrow morning."

"I don't even know how to read a screenplay," Carrie replied quickly, looking for a way to end the conversation.

"I'm sending it to you anyway," Adam declared. "What's the address?"

Carrie reluctantly gave him Graham and Claudia's address.

"You read it," Adam instructed Carrie. "That's all I ask. Will you do that?"

"Okay," Carrie agreed.

"And if you see the brilliance of it—and I really believe you will—then if you want to, you could show it to Graham Perry."

"I could *what*?" Carrie asked.

"The money would mean nothing to him," Adam said, "just like it wouldn't mean anything to Emma."

"Look, I'll read your screenplay," Carrie said, "but I'm not showing it to Graham and I'm not asking him to put money into it."

"But—"

"Sorry," Carrie said firmly. "He's my employer. I could never do that."

There was silence on the phone.

"You think I crossed the bounds of good taste, huh?" Adam said, a trace of irony in his voice.

"Frankly, yes."

"You're right," Adam said softly. "I have. But art isn't about good manners, or whose feelings might get hurt. I'm sorry, but that's just the way it is. Anyway, thanks for saying you'll read it."

"Okay, but—" Carrie began.

But Adam had already hung up.

NINE

"Okay, everyone," Ian Templeton called to the members of his band, Lord Whitehead and the Zit People, "we're going to try the new tune I just wrote. Here are the lyrics. I call it 'Evil Twin.'"

From their post at the stairs in the Templetons' house that led down to the music room, Carrie, Emma, and Sam traded significant looks. Chloe snuggled into Carrie's lap, watching the band rehearsal with rapt attention.

"Uh-oh," Carrie muttered. "Why do I get the feeling he wrote this about Becky?"

"And why do I get this feeling that the you-know-what is about to hit the old fan," Sam added.

It was late the next afternoon. Claudia

and Graham had left for New York, which meant that Carrie was pretty much housebound. Since Becky and Allie were backup singers for the Zits, Sam had had to drive them to rehearsal from the club, then she decided to stay to keep Carrie company. And since the Hewitts were on a picnic with their kids, Emma was free to come hang out with her friends.

"Hey, I don't like this song," Becky said, scanning the lyrics.

"Too bad," Ian said. "I'm the leader of this band, and what I say goes."

"'She's bad to the bone/ She'll do you in/ She'll leave you all alone/ She's the evil twin'?" Marcus Woods, a member of the band, read out loud.

"Does that make me the good twin?" Allie asked with a bright grin.

"Who says it's about Becky?" Ian asked snottily.

Becky walked over to Ian. "Can we handle this privately instead of in front of the whole band?"

"Believe it or not, Becky, this isn't about you," Ian tossed off, running his fingers through the front of his hair.

"It is, too," Becky insisted, trying to keep her voice low. But Carrie and everyone else could easily hear every word she was saying. "Look, all I'm doing is going to a party with a bunch of friends."

"At that guy's camp," Ian snapped.

"Well, so what?" Becky asked. "There are lots of people at that camp!"

"But you're going because he invited you," Ian maintained.

"Look, it's just a party," Becky said. "It's not such a big deal. I'm not deserting you—"

"Ever since you started that C.I.T. job, you never have any time for me—"

"Well, it's a job!" Becky exclaimed. "What am I supposed to do, quit?"

"You're just using it as an excuse—"

"I am not!" Becky cried. "Besides, you could have been a C.I.T., too. I asked you to apply. I begged you, even. You said you'd rather have pins stuck under your nails, or something like that—"

"I'm a musician!" Ian yelled. "I don't have time for that stupid stuff! I thought you were serious about music, too—"

"I am serious!" Becky yelled back. "But there's more to life than this band, you know—"

"We're taking the song from the top," Ian called, ignoring Becky even though by this time she was standing in his face. Now he turned back to her. "Backups, when we get to the chorus, you two just keep chanting, 'I'm evil, evil, I'm wicked, wicked.' Got that?"

"So what's this whole list of stuff at the bottom of the page?" Donald Zuckerman, another band member, asked. "It says global warming, violence, AIDS, pollution . . ."

"Those are other evils," Ian said. "The backups are going to chant that during the instrumental section."

Sam snorted back a laugh, and Carrie nudged her in the ribs. "Instrumental," in this case, meant banging sticks against hulked-out appliances, what the band called "industrial music."

"This is totally insulting," Becky said. "I'm not singing it." She held the lyric sheet out to Ian.

"If you don't sing it, you're not in the band," Ian snapped.

"So? Who cares?" Becky yelled. "Why is this band run like a dictatorship anyway?"

"Because—" Ian began.

Becky grabbed his sleeve. "Can we just please talk privately? Please?"

Ian struggled a moment. "All right," he finally said in a stiff voice. "Band, take ten." Carrie, Emma, and Sam moved aside so that Ian and Becky could go upstairs.

"Well, I guess this means I'll be singing lead," Allie chirped.

Chloe looked up at Carrie. "Are Ian and Becky having a fight?"

"Maybe," Carrie replied.

"I want to have my own band, too," Chloe said.

Carrie laughed and ruffled Chloe's hair. "You do, huh?"

Chloe nodded. "Just like Salt 'N' Pepa." She began to dance around on the step, wriggling her tiny hips. "Oh, baby, oh, baby," she sang.

Emma looked horrified. "What happened to *Sesame Street* and Barney?"

Carrie just sighed and shook her head. "How about if we go upstairs, Chloe?" she suggested. "We could make some lemonade for everyone, okay?"

"Okay," Chloe agreed, stopping middance.

Carrie took the little girl by the hand and everyone tromped upstairs. It took forever to make the lemonade—Chloe insisted on squeezing the lemons herself—but finally Carrie took the pitcher back downstairs and Chloe stayed down there, telling everyone her recipe for the drink. Ian and Becky were still off somewhere, fighting.

"You know, having kids is a major pain in the butt," Sam said as she downed her own glass of lemonade upstairs in the kitchen.

"I'm sure the rewards are great," Emma said.

Carrie eyed them both. *There is definitely still tension in the air between the two of them,* she realized.

"I doubt it," Sam said, putting her long legs up on the kitchen table. She turned to Emma. "So, did you call Adam yet?"

"You certainly don't beat around the bush, do you?" Carrie asked, putting the extra lemons back into the refrigerator.

Sam shrugged. "What's the point?"

I have to tell Emma that Adam called me, Carrie thought. *I don't know how I got in the middle of all this!*

"I hardly slept last night," Emma said in a low voice. She gave Sam a hard look. "If you think this is easy for me, you're wrong."

"I don't think it's easy—" Sam began.

"I really care about Adam," Emma continued.

"I know you do," Sam replied. "But isn't it just possible that Adam cares about you *and* about his screenplay?" Sam asked, setting her cowboy-boot–clad feet back on the floor. "Would anything be so wrong with that?"

"No," Emma said. "And maybe I'm being too sensitive about this. But once I tell Adam I'm not putting any money into his movie, I truly don't think our relationship will ever be the same again."

"That's your choice," Sam said with a shrug.

"No, he made the choice," Emma said, "when he decided to ask me for money."

"I have to tell you both something," Carrie said, sitting down with them at the table. "I got a call from Adam last night."

Emma and Sam stared at her, surprise etched on their faces.

"What did he want?" Emma finally managed.

"He wanted me to talk you into putting up the money for his movie," Carrie admitted. Sam blanched. "I'm sorry, Sam, but that's the truth."

"Why didn't he call me?" Sam asked.

"He said Emma wouldn't listen to you because you're family."

"I can't believe he dragged you into this," Emma said.

"There's more," Carrie said with a sigh. "He insisted on sending me a copy of his screenplay so I could judge its worth for myself—"

"Well, that's good," Sam interrupted. "He wanted you to talk to Emma only if you agreed that his script was worth it—"

"True," Carrie conceded. "But he also wanted me to give it to Graham and ask him to invest in it."

Silence filled the kitchen.

"You're kidding," Emma finally managed to say.

"Unfortunately, I'm not," Carrie said.

Sam folded her arms. "What is the big deal here?" she asked. "He's not a serial killer, you know. He's just trying to raise money for his movie."

"He's trying to use us," Emma explained patiently.

"According to what Adam's told me, everyone gets their stuff financed through connections when they start out," Sam said. "And if the movie is a success, all of a sudden those same people think the filmmaker is this wonderful human being instead of thinking he's some jerk they helped out."

"I just don't see it that way," Emma said quietly.

"Well, that's obvious," Sam replied dryly.

"I didn't tell you about his phone call so that the two of you would start fighting about it again!" Carrie exclaimed.

"We're not fighting!" Sam and Emma both snapped at the same time.

Chloe came running into the kitchen. "Why are you guys yelling?"

"We're sorry," Carrie said, giving her a hug. "We were discussing something and we got carried away."

"Well, Ian and Becky are out in the backyard by the pool, and they were yelling really loud," Chloe reported importantly, grabbing Carrie's hand.

"They're having a disagreement, I think," Carrie explained.

"I think it's a fight," Chloe said with a shrug. "A really, really big one. And I think Becky won."

"Why do you think that?" Emma asked her.

"Oh, because she just pushed Ian into the swimming pool with all his clothes on," Chloe reported nonchalantly.

Carrie ran toward the family room, heading for the backyard just as Becky marched in through the sliding glass doors.

"I quit!" she yelled.

"You're fired!" Ian yelled after her, water dripping from him everywhere.

"I'll get you a towel," Carrie offered.

"I don't need a towel!" Ian snapped.

"But you're dripping all over everything," Carrie pointed out.

"So? Maybe I like to drip!" Ian yelled. Then he marched toward the stairs leading up to the bedrooms.

"Uh, Ian, your band is still downstairs," Carrie reminded him. "Do you want me to tell them anything?"

"Tell them Becky is out of the band!" Ian yelled.

"I heard that!" Becky yelled, and she marched over to Ian. "You can have your band, Ian. You think you can control everything, including my life, well—"

"Emma, you're wrong!" Carrie heard Sam yell from the kitchen.

The angry voices of Emma and Sam and Becky and Ian all blended together. Carrie put her hands over her ears. And all she could think was *I want Billy!*

*　*　*

That evening Carrie got her wish. Chloe was in bed, asleep, and Ian was reading in his room, when the doorbell rang.

"Hi there," Billy said, grinning down at her.

Wordlessly she wrapped her arms around his neck and just stood there, inhaling his special fragrance.

"Yeah, I missed you, too," Billy said, holding her close. "Can I come in?"

"Sure," Carrie said, holding open the door. They went into the family room and sat close together on the couch. "What a day," Carrie said. "Everyone was fighting. How was yours?"

"Great, actually," Billy said. "Pres and I wrote a new tune, and now Jake and Erin are starting to write together."

"Do you think it's harder for artists to have relationships?" Carrie mused, leaning against Billy's shoulder.

"Got me," Billy said.

"I mean, if a person puts so much energy into their art, how do they have enough left over to put into the relationship?" Carrie clarified.

Billy raised his eyebrows. "Have I been neglecting you?"

"I wasn't talking about you," Carrie assured him.

"Well, then, I don't know," Billy said, kissing Carrie's forehead. "Because I've never been anyone but me."

"Ha-ha," Carrie said dryly. She stared out into the distance for a moment. "What do you think would happen if one person was an artist and the other person didn't think the artist had any talent?" Carrie finally asked.

Now Billy really turned to look at her. "Who are we talking about here?"

"Let's keep it theoretical for now," Carrie decided.

"Okay," Billy agreed. "Well, I think that would be really tough, maybe even impossible."

"That's what I figured," Carrie said glumly.

"You're sure you didn't decide I don't have any talent?" Billy asked her.

Carrie laughed. "I think you're filled with first-class grade-A talent, I promise."

Billy leaned close and kissed her ear softly. "Talent for what?"

"Music," Carrie said, a smile playing at her lips.

"Is that all?" he pressed.

"Maybe," Carrie said, a teasing look on her face. "I'll never tell."

"Oh, don't worry," Billy said, "you already told me."

She raised her eyebrows.

"Body language speaks volumes," he pointed out.

"Oh, aren't we smug," Carrie laughed.

Billy grabbed her in a tight bear hug and then loosened his grip. "I'm not smug. I'm happy. I'm in love."

"Me, too," Carrie said softly.

"I really want to—" Billy began.

"Hey, Car, is there anything to eat?" Ian asked, padding into the family room in his bare feet.

"There's some leftover pizza you can nuke," Carrie told him.

"Oh, hi, Billy," Ian said.

"How's it going?"

"Basically, life sucks," Ian said, and he left for the kitchen.

"Trouble in love-land," Carrie explained. "Emma and Sam are fighting, too. And Emma's all nuts over something that happened with Adam. And she doesn't know what's going on with Kurt. . . ."

"This sounds like a soap opera," Billy commented.

Carrie laughed. "And not even a good soap opera at that!" She nuzzled closer to him. "I am just so lucky," she murmured. "My life is so perfect."

"I really want to be alone with you again," Billy said. "Soon."

"That's what I want, too," Carrie agreed. "But until Claudia and Graham get back from New York, there's no way."

"There's always the Sam solution," Billy reminded her, wriggling his eyebrows playfully. "Graham and Claudia's bed . . ."

"And then we could write an article for a tabloid afterward," Carrie said, "'I Had Sex in a Superstar's Bed.'"

"Sorry, sweetheart, the story wouldn't sell unless the superstar was in the bed with you," Billy pointed out.

"But I don't want the superstar," Carrie said softly. "I want you."

Billy looked up. "Thanks, God. You sent me a great woman."

"I'm going to bed," Ian announced from the doorway, chewing on a slice of pizza. He looked over at Billy. "Take my advice, man, stay away from the ladies if you want to be happy."

Billy nodded and tried not to laugh.

"You can't be an artist and a boyfriend, no way," Ian mumbled, and he headed for the stairs.

"Poor kid," Carrie said.

"Hmmm, let me see, should I take his advice?" Billy pretended to muse.

"No," Carrie said, pulling on the collar of Billy's shirt to bring him closer to her.

"Okay," Billy agreed, and he began to kiss her passionately.

"Uh, this isn't cool," Carrie finally said breathlessly when she could manage to pull her lips away from his.

"Yeah, I guess not," Billy agreed, his breath ragged. "We need to be alone."

"Soon," Carrie agreed.

"Soon," Billy echoed. He got up. "Which

means I'd better leave before I tear your clothes off right here and now."

Carrie walked him to the door. She sniffed the night air and stared up at the starry sky. "It's beautiful out," she whispered.

"Wait until I show you the night sky in Seattle," Billy said. "You've never seen anything like it."

"I can't wait," Carrie said.

They kissed good-bye one last time, and Carrie watched Billy drive off, until he disappeared into the night.

TEN

"Ian!" Chloe cried. "Quit it!"

"I was here first!" Ian shouted at his sister.

"So what?" Chloe shouted.

"So everything!"

"Gimme it!" Chloe screamed.

"No way!" Ian bellowed.

Carrie, who was in the kitchen preparing lunch for the two of them, got up from the table to see what all the shouting was about.

It was the next day, and with Graham and Claudia in New York, Carrie still had complete charge of Ian and Chloe.

And almost from the minute their parents left, Carrie thought grimly, *both of them have been totally obnoxious. Usu-*

ally it's just one or the other. Why did they have to pick this time to both go off the deep end?

As Carrie walked from the kitchen into the family room, the battle escalated to near-epic proportions.

"I was here first!" Ian repeated loudly. "Get out of here!"

"Not fair!" Chloe cried in her little voice. "I'm going to tell on you!"

"I'm so scared," Ian taunted nastily.

"You're mean to me!" Chloe yelled. "I hate you!"

"Boo-hoo, boo-hoo," Ian whined, imitating Chloe crying.

Carrie strode into the room, a determined look on her face. She saw Ian sitting on the plush couch, cradling the remote control for the big-screen TV. And Chloe was standing right at Ian's side. On the television, Carrie saw, was a baseball game.

"Okay," Carrie said forcefully, "what's this all about?"

"I was here first," Ian said quickly, "before *she* came in. I'm watching a baseball game. Obviously. Red Sox."

"I wanna watch MTV!" Chloe cried.

"Too bad," Ian sneered.

"I want MTV!" Chloe whined.

There are three different televisions in this house, Carrie thought. *They would have to decide at this very instant that they both have to watch on the big screen, wouldn't they?*

"Ian," Carrie suggested, thinking she might have better luck reasoning with him than with the little girl, "why don't you go watch upstairs?"

"Why doesn't she?" Ian asked. "I was here first, wasn't I?"

"Yes, but—"

"I want MTV!" Chloe whined again.

Suddenly Ian lost his temper. "I'll give you your stupid MTV!" he shouted, jumping up and starting to chase Chloe away as Carrie watched, dumbfounded. Chloe ran with surprising speed as Ian chased her into the next room—Graham's library— and then out the door that led into the attached garage.

"Good!" Ian yelled as Chloe closed the garage door behind her. "You'll never come back in. Never, never, never, never,

never!" And Ian held the door so Chloe couldn't open it. Carrie could hear Chloe burst into hysterical crying on the other side of the door.

Oh, brother, Carrie thought as she hurried into the study. *I can't believe this is happening.*

"Ian!" Carrie shouted. "Let your sister back in!"

"Okay, okay," Ian replied, taking his hands off the door.

Unfortunately, at just that moment Chloe chose to push the door open with all her might. And even though she was only five years old, she pushed hard, and the door swung open with amazing speed.

Smack into the glass wall of one of Graham's prize twenty-gallon aquariums.

Crack! The handle of the garage door went right through the glass. Twenty gallons of water—and about two dozen freshwater tropical fish came gushing out of the aquarium onto the wooden floor of Graham's library.

I can't believe this is happening, Carrie thought quickly. *This is not happening.*

"Uh-oh," Chloe said in a small voice,

surveying the mess she'd made. "We're gonna be in trouble."

No kidding, Carrie thought to herself as she began issuing orders to Ian and Chloe, which the two kids obeyed immediately, as if there never had been a big fight between them.

Ian ran for the mop, Chloe ran and got newspapers. Carrie, meanwhile, started scooping guppies, mollies, and neon tetras up with a net and dropping them into another fresh-water aquarium. She hoped they were compatible, but she didn't have much choice.

It took almost an hour to clean the whole mess up.

When they were done, Chloe insisted she had to change her clothes because of the "fish ick" on them, which gave Carrie a moment alone with Ian.

"Well, that was quite a scene," Carrie said as she and Ian sat for a moment in the kitchen.

"She's such a spoiled brat," Ian said.

"Ian, she's five and you're thirteen," Carrie reminded him gently.

"So?" Ian said stubbornly, kicking the heel of his sneaker into the linoleum.

"Look, we don't have to talk about this if you don't want to," Carrie began, "but I think you're upset about Becky and you're taking it out on Chloe."

Ian didn't say anything, he just kept slamming his heel into the floor.

"I think Becky really cares about you, Ian," Carrie said, "even though it might not feel that way to you."

Finally, Ian raised his head and looked at her. Carrie had never seen him look so desolate. "If she really cared about me, then she wouldn't do anything to hurt me," he finally said. "So maybe she never really cared about me at all."

Ian disappeared to his room, and Carrie just sat there, thinking. *That's just how Emma feels about Adam,* she realized. *Just exactly.*

"So that's the scene of the crime," Carrie said as she finished telling Emma the story of Ian and Chloe's fight. She pointed to the shattered aquarium.

Emma shook her head. "I feel lucky. The Hewitt kids have been little angels lately."

It was two hours after the disaster with Graham's aquarium, and Emma had stopped over for a little while. She had called earlier and talked to Carrie about the situation with Adam—she was ready to call Adam and tell him about her decision not to finance his movie, but she wanted to do it with Carrie nearby, for moral support.

"Ian is so bummed out about Becky," Carrie said, leading the way into the kitchen. "He's really, really hurt."

"You never get over your first love," Emma murmured.

Carrie cocked her head to one side. "Are you talking about him or you?"

"Both, probably," Emma admitted. "I'll probably never feel about anyone the way I felt about Kurt."

"Felt, as in past tense, or feel, as in present tense?" Carrie wondered, setting a bowl of popcorn on the table.

Emma sighed. "Well, if I knew the

answer to that, my life would be a lot simpler, wouldn't it?" She grabbed a few pieces of popcorn and nibbled them delicately. "I dreamed about Kurt last night," she admitted. "I dreamed he—wait, where are the kids? I don't want them walking in on this."

"You may find this hard to believe," Carrie said, reaching for a handful of popcorn, "but even as we speak Ian's upstairs watching the end of the Red Sox game, and Chloe's watching MTV in the family room. Just as I suggested in the first place!" They both laughed.

"You ready to call Adam?" Carrie asked Emma as they wandered into Graham's office, where there was a speakerphone. "Because I'm going to be taking the kids bowling soon."

"Not really," Emma sighed.

"If it helps at all, I did get a chance to look through his screenplay," Carrie offered. "I didn't think it was very good."

"That helps some," Emma replied, "but not much. Let's just get this over with." She went over to the speakerphone, took out a piece of paper with Adam's number in Los Angeles written on it, and dialed it, being careful to charge the call to her calling card. Then she sat down with Carrie on the couch in Graham's office and waited for Adam to answer.

"Hello?" Adam said, answering the phone on the second ring.

"Adam?" Emma said hesitant. "It's Emma."

"Emma," Adam breathed. "You didn't need to identify yourself. I'd know your voice anywhere."

"I'm here with Carrie," Emma said carefully, glancing over at her friend, "on the speakerphone."

"Very Hollywood," Adam commented archly, "the speakerphone. Hi, Carrie. The screenplay arrived okay, right?"

"Hi," Carrie said without much enthusiasm. "It did."

"And?" Adam asked hopefully.

"And I didn't get a chance to really read it thoroughly yet," she explained. She shrugged helplessly at Emma.

"Remember what we talked about when you read it, okay?" Adam reminded Carrie.

"We didn't talk about anything," Carrie said. "Except that I told you I won't give it to Graham."

"Please," Adam said, "don't make that decision until you've really lived with the script."

Carrie rolled her eyes at Emma.

"Adam," Emma said, taking over the conversation, "I wanted to talk to you about financing your movie."

Carrie winced. *Bad phrasing,* she thought. *It sounds as if Emma wants to finance it!*

"Great!" Adam cried. "Emma, that's so wonderful, I'm so thankful, you'll never regret it, never!"

Emma's hand went to her forehead and she closed her eyes. "Adam, I think you've misunderstood me."

Adam laughed. "Emma, you're hilarious."

Emma looked over at Carrie, who shrugged at her.

"I'm serious," Emma said quietly.

"What are you talking about?" Adam asked, a tinge of fear beginning to color his words.

"Well," Emma said slowly, "I think your screenplay has a lot of potential, but—"

"But what?" Adam said, his whole tone of voice changing.

"But . . . I just don't think it's the kind of investment I want to make now, Adam. You know, the film business is very risky," Emma said quickly, "and—"

"You hate it," Adam said in a flat voice.

"No!" Emma cried. "I think it has a lot of potential!"

"But not enough for you to invest in it," Adam surmised sadly.

"But I don't think my investing in it would be a good idea, anyway," Emma admitted.

"The problem, Emma," Adam said in a biting tone, "is the people with the talent don't have the money, and the people with the money don't have the talent!"

"What's that supposed to mean?" Emma asked. Carrie knew exactly what it was supposed to mean.

"It means that you don't have any taste!" Adam exploded. "And I was so sure that you did!"

"That is totally unfair," Emma replied somewhat hotly.

"Well, the truth hurts sometimes," Adam snapped.

"Look, just because I don't like your screenplay enough to want to put my money into it docsn't mean I have no taste," Emma pointed out.

"So, why don't you tell me what's wrong with it, if you have such elevated taste?" Adam asked bitterly.

"Adam, that's not the point—" Emma began.

"Of course it's the point," Adam insisted. "Enlighten me, why don't you. Give me notes, point by point, slowly, so that I can jot everything down—"

"Okay, I will!" Emma finally exploded. "I'll give you one big fat note! Your screenplay is awful! It's boring! And pretentious!"

Carrie put her head in her hands and sighed. *This isn't exactly going well,* she thought to herself.

There was a long beat of silence.

"Well, so much for my beautiful muse

sticking by me through thick and thin," Adam said, trying to cover his hurt with levity.

"Oh, Adam, I'm sorry I lost it like that," Emma said with a sigh, "it's just that—"

"No need to apologize," Adam said. "You could use a little more honesty in your life, Emma Cresswell. Good manners aren't everything, you know."

"I wish you'd never asked me to put money into this," Emma said bitterly. "I really do. It wasn't very fair of you."

"Well, it's a little too late for that, isn't it," Adam said. "Anyway, this is good. Because now I know that the whole fantasy I had about you and me was just that . . . a fantasy."

"Oh, Adam—" Emma began.

"This is my art, Emma," Adam said heavily. "If you don't get it, how could you possibly get me?"

Emma was speechless, her face pale.

"Mark my words, Emma Cresswell— the day will come when you will be sorry," Adam said, his voice low and intense.

Emma took a deep breath. "Listen, Adam," she said. "I might be completely wrong about it. If it's a really good screenplay, you'll be able to find other investors for it. I just hope that we can stay friends."

"Friends?" Adam echoed. He laughed bitterly. "I thought we were heading toward being much more than friends."

"Maybe we were," Emma said quietly. "But I just can't lie to you about this."

"No, I guess you can't," Adam said sadly. "I guess who I fell for wasn't really you at all, it was who I wanted you to be."

"Adam," Emma began tentatively, "look, I have to ask you this, because you don't even sound like yourself. Are you . . . doing drugs or something? Speed?"

Adam laughed harshly. "Everyone at film school does speed. How else do you think we can get everything done?"

"But you hate drugs!" Emma declared. "You told me so yourself."

"Chill out, Emma," Adam replied. "Copping a hit of speed now and then doesn't make me a drug addict."

"It's changing your personality," Emma said quietly.

Adam sighed into the phone. "This *is* my personality, Emma. I'm sorry if you thought I was someone else."

And he hung up the phone.

Both girls just sat there, stunned.

"He hung up on me," Emma finally said.

"Maybe it was the speed talking, plus he's hurt," Carrie pointed out. "Maybe he'll get over it."

Emma shook her head no. "This is just what I was afraid would happen. He feels like I can't reject the art without rejecting the artist."

"That's just what Billy said . . ." Carrie mused.

"Film means so much to him," Emma said. "How could we have gone further with our relationship if I didn't respect his art?"

"I honestly don't know," Carrie replied. *And I'm so lucky that Billy really is talented,* she added to herself.

"And he's just starting out. Why does

he think this screenplay has to be so important? Maybe he'll get better." Emma stood up. "Let's go get a drink, okay?"

"Sure," Carrie agreed.

They walked into the kitchen and Carrie got out a pitcher of iced tea and poured them both a glass. "For what it's worth, I'm really sorry things worked out like they did for the two of you," Carrie said, handing Emma a glass of tea.

"I can't believe it," Emma said, sitting at the table. She put her tea down and stared at the glass as if she could find some answers in the amber liquid. "How did my life get so complicated?" she asked.

Carrie didn't say anything, she just sat down next to her and silently drank her tea.

Emma's purse lay on the table. She reached into the side pocket and took out a folded piece of paper.

"What is it?" Carrie asked.

"A letter from Kurt that I got today," Emma said. "I told you my life was complicated. Read it. I want to know what you think."

Carrie reached over and took the piece of paper, unfolded it, and began to read.

Dear Emma,

I got your last letter. It sounds like things are going well for you. I'm glad.

It's weird out here in Michigan. I am preparing to go to Colorado Springs and the Air Force Academy by doing a lot of swimming and also a lot of running—I'm up to six miles a day, right at daybreak. Sounds like fun, doesn't it? I'm boning up on my math, too, because I know there're a lot of technical courses.

But I'm also thinking about everything all the time. I keep playing out our last phone conversation over and over in my head. And then I wonder— will we ever really be able to talk to each other again?

Sometimes I can't believe that I'm going to the Air Force Academy. Some days I wake up not wanting to go. Some days I have this fantasy, that I'm back on Sunset Island, walking on the beach in the evening by myself, and I see you, far off in the distance, wearing one of those white dresses you have, walking slowly toward me.

Stupid, isn't it? Because you're there, and I'm here, and so much water has gone under the bridge. So I start thinking that I have to move on, get you out of my system. And the Academy will be a great place to do it. Then I go to sleep, and I dream about you again, and I think I'll die if I don't get to hold you in my arms one more time.

Kurt

Carrie looked up when she was done reading. "Wow."

"So?" Emma said, an anxious look on her face. "What do you think?"

Carrie gave Emma a puzzled look. "I'm not sure," she said honestly, taking a sip of iced tea before she spoke. "But one thing is for sure."

"What's that?" Emma asked.

"This isn't the same Kurt Ackerman who was so mad at you he couldn't stay another minute on Sunset Island." She looked over at her friend. "What is it *you* want, Em?"

Emma took a deep breath, and tears came to her eyes. "Another chance," she finally whispered. "I want another chance."

ELEVEN

"I don't get it," Carrie said as she sat up and brushed some sand off of her legs.

"What's that?" Billy asked her, still prone on the big beach blanket the two of them had brought with them.

"When I'm home with them alone, they're totally impossible, but now . . ." Carrie whispered, gesturing toward Ian and Chloe, who were engaged in the building of a monstrous sand castle twenty yards away from where Carrie and Billy were talking.

It was the next day—the last day Carrie was going to have Ian and Chloe alone, without Graham and Claudia. Billy had suggested that all four of them go to the beach together, a suggestion to which Ian and Chloe had readily agreed.

"Will you play airplane with me?" Chloe had asked Billy.

"Till you can't fly anymore," Billy had promised as the little girl chortled with glee. And then, when Billy had told Ian that he would work with him on the lyrics to any new song he wanted, Ian was as convinced as Chloe had been.

So the four of them had gone together to the main beach, which was, as usual, totally packed with tourists. But they'd managed to arrive fairly early—before noon—and squeezed into a space on the sand between a family visiting from Quebec, chattering away in French, and a group of elderly men who would periodically jump up all together, give a loud shout, run down to the ocean, and dive in.

"But now?" Billy prompted Carrie, dropping some sand lightly on her bare arm.

"Now they're acting like angels," Carrie said, brushing the sand off her arm.

"I guess it's just my mature masculine attention keeping them in line," Billy said in a deep baritone. He puffed out his chest with mock self-importance.

"I guess it's just being at the beach," Carrie said, pulling on Billy's ponytail.

"Hey, come build the castle with us, Billy!" Chloe called to him excitedly.

"In a little while," Billy called back. He turned to Carrie. "Ah-ha! You notice Chloe called for me and not for you."

"Good!" Carrie said with a laugh. "You go and I'll read this novel I've been trying to finish for a week."

"I could find other ways to occupy you," Billy said, kissing Carrie's cheek.

"Not on a public beach, you couldn't," Carrie said, pushing him away.

"This is going to be the biggest sand castle ever built!" Chloe cried, jumping up and down.

Carrie smiled fondly at the little girl. "Someday I want children," Carrie said dreamily.

"Someday as in soon?" Billy asked, looking nervous.

"No," Carrie said, "so you can wipe that petrified look off your face. Someday as in down-the-road-when-I'm-ready."

"Boys or girls?" Billy asked.

"Two of each, how's that?" Carrie asked.

"That's four, which is a whole lot of kids," Billy said. He lay down on his stomach, and Carrie lay down next to him. "You really want four?"

"Who knows?" Carrie asked. "I don't even know what it's like to have one. Maybe the fantasy is better than the reality."

"I think my mom wanted girls," Billy said quietly. "Instead, she got two strapping boys—not what she bargained for at all."

"But she loves you—" Carrie began.

"Sure, I guess," Billy agreed. "But you'd have to know my mom. For example, she keeps a room in our house all decorated like a little girl's room."

"Are you serious?" Carrie asked.

Billy nodded. "She had a miscarriage a long time ago, and the doctors told her it would have been a girl. Believe it or not, she actually keeps a room fixed up for her."

Carrie shivered. "That's kind of gruesome."

"I guess I'm used to it," Billy said. "Anyway, Mom explains the whole thing by pointing out her antique doll collection. She says she created an environment just for them. That sounds a whole lot less bizarre, huh?"

"Yes," Carrie agreed. *My parents are so normal compared to that!* Carrie thought to herself. She reached out and ran her hand over Billy's arm. "Do you want kids?" she asked softly.

"Yeah, I think so," Billy said. "But in my mind I'm as successful as Graham Perry before I start a family."

"What if you aren't?" Carrie asked curiously.

"I can't even deal with thinking about that," Billy said.

"You mean you'd give up having kids if you didn't become a superstar?" Carrie asked with concern.

Billy smiled at her. "When I look at you, Carrie, I think having kids would be a blast, no matter what. Does that answer your question?"

"As a matter of fact, yes," Carrie said. She gave him a quick kiss, then she lay

185

back down. "You know what I'm really glad about?" she murmured, enjoying the feel of the hot sun on her back.

"What?"

"That you're so talented," Carrie said. Then she told him what had happened between Emma and Adam the day before.

"That's a drag," Billy commented. "But it's like I said, if you don't respect the art, how do you respect the artist?"

"So, do you respect my photography?" Carrie asked him.

"You know I do."

"What if it were going to take me . . . oh, I don't know . . . far away from you. To England, or Asia," Carrie posed. "How would you feel then?"

"I'd feel like I'd want you to take pictures somewhere where you could come home to me at night," Billy told her.

"You go on tour," Carrie pointed out. "I won't always be able to go with you."

"I wouldn't expect you to," Billy said. "Of course, if you wanted to, I'd be thrilled."

"Right answer!" Carrie said with a laugh.

Billy put his arm around her. "Some-day, Car, it's just going to be you and me and Slick."

"Slick?" Carrie echoed.

"Our kid, Slick," Billy said.

"You want to name a child Slick?" Carrie asked.

"After Grace Slick from the Jefferson Airplane," Billy explained. "Great name, huh? And it works for a boy or a girl."

Carrie stared at him. "I can't tell if you're serious or not."

"Frank Zappa named his kid Moon Unit," Billy reminded her. "Slick is tame compared to that."

"Maybe we'd better table this discussion for a few years," Carrie suggested. She sat up and stretched, checking on the kids. "Look at that, they're still building the sand castle, and Ian is helping Chloe build a moat."

Billy sat up, too. "Very sweet."

Carrie looked over at him. "What's going to happen to us this fall?" she asked him softly.

Billy reached into the cooler and took

out two cans of fruit juice. He handed one to Carrie. "What brought that on?"

"The fact that I'm so happy," Carrie said, "and I don't want anything to change."

"I'll come visit you at Yale," Billy said. "As often as I can." He took a long guzzle of the juice. "When do classes start?"

"I don't want to think about it," Carrie made a face. "But in early September."

"I'm there in mid-September," Billy promised. "Maybe we can even get our booking agent to set a few dates for the Flirts in New Haven!"

"I'd love that," Carrie said, her eyes shining.

"But I want you to visit Seattle before that," Billy said. He gave a short laugh. "After you see how bizarre my family is, you might not be planning a future with me!"

"Nothing's going to change my mind about that," Carrie vowed.

"Maybe we could take a few days at the end of the summer," Billy said, "when you're done at the Templetons but before you have to head to New Haven."

"That's a great idea," Carrie said. "But

I promised Graham and Claudia that I'd stay on the island until Labor Day this year—it's what they wanted."

"Well, if we can't do it in September, we'll do it for Thanksgiving," Billy planned. "Evan should be home on leave then—we all try to get together."

But I always spend Thanksgiving with my family, Carrie thought. *They'd feel terrible if I weren't there.* But she didn't say anything. She just smiled. *It'll all work out. Billy and I love each other.*

"I'm off kiddie duty now, man," Ian said as he walked over to them and flopped down on the blanket.

"It looked to me like you were having fun," Billy pointed out.

Ian shrugged and reached into the cooler for a cold drink. "I haven't been exactly nice to Chloe lately." He took a long drink from the can. "I figure if she's got any hope of growing up with better values than Becky, I'd better start working with her now."

"You ready to play airplane?" Chloe asked, running over to Billy and jumping into his lap.

189

"I sure am," Billy said. He jumped up and picked the little girl up in his arms. She giggled and squealed as he ran down the sandy beach with her.

Ian looked at Carrie. "Are you and Billy in love?"

"Yes," Carrie said, smiling as she watched Billy with the little girl.

"I've decided I'm never going to allow myself to feel anything again," Ian said. "What's the point? You just get hurt."

"If you don't feel anything, you can't feel bad," Carrie said, "but you can't feel good either."

Ian sighed and looked out at the ocean. "It's just not worth it, Carrie. If you love someone, they have too much power over you. They can break your heart."

Carrie couldn't think of a thing to say, so she just put her arm around Ian's slender shoulders and hoped he knew how much she cared.

Ah, Carrie thought as she stretched out on her bed. *An hour of peace before I go to sleep. Thank goodness Claudia and Graham come back tomorrow. I think I should take Billy's advice—every time they go out of town and I'm left with the kids, I should demand combat-duty pay!*

Billy had dropped Carrie, Ian, and Chloe back at the Templetons' after their long day at the beach—the idea, he'd said with a grin, was that Chloe and Ian would be so tired out from the beach that they'd want to go to sleep early.

The strategy had worked. Chloe wanted Carrie to read her stories, but Ian had gone off to his own room. Then, mid-story, Chloe had fallen asleep on the couch, and Carrie had taken the little girl up to her room and tucked her into bed.

Ahhhhh, Carrie thought again blissfully, reaching for the book she'd been reading, *maybe I'll be able to read for a while. In peace!*

She'd just settled back on the bed and read the first page, when the doorbell rang.

Who could that be? she thought to herself, a little alarmed. *We're not expecting anyone.* She took a quick look out her window to see if she could see a familiar car.

The Flirts' van.

"Billy!" Carrie cried happily. "What a sweetheart!" She quickly ran downstairs and opened the front door.

"You just kill me," Carrie said with a laugh. "You couldn't stay away from me, huh?" She reached up for him, and then she noticed the horrible look on his face.

"Billy?" she asked, her voice faint. "Billy, what is it?"

He just stood there, looking dazed.

"What's the matter?" Carrie cried, grabbing his arm. "What's wrong?"

"Carrie," Billy finally said, "something terrible has happened."

Oh, my God, Carrie thought quickly. *What could have happened?*

Carrie led Billy into the family room. "Is it Sly?" she asked, referring to the Flirts' original drummer, who had been diagnosed with AIDS, and was currently with his family in Maryland.

"No," Billy replied. He sat heavily on the couch. "It's not Sly."

"Well, what then?" Carrie demanded. "Please, talk to me. You're scaring the life out of me!"

Billy took a deep breath. "It's my dad."

Carrie's hand flew to her mouth. "Is he—?"

"He's alive," Billy said, his voice flat. "For the moment anyway. My mom called me. There was an accident at Dad's shop. He was working on a car that was jacked up on a lift. The car fell on him."

"Oh, no!"

"There are massive internal injuries," Billy continued in the same colorless voice. "The doctor told my mom the odds are only fifty-fifty that he'll make it."

Carrie reached for Billy's hand and held it tight. "What can I do to help?"

Billy wiped his hand over his eyes wearily. "Even if he makes it, the situation is really bad," Billy continued, not answering Carrie's question. "Both his legs are broken, his pelvis is shattered, he might never walk again." He looked at Carrie. "I just can't believe this is really happening."

"You're in shock," Carrie said.

"I have to go home, Carrie."

"Of course you do," Carrie said, holding his hand as tightly as she could.

"No, you don't understand," Billy said in the same scary, dull voice. "I don't know when I'll be back. I don't know *if* I'll be back."

Carrie gulped hard. *Please,* she prayed, *don't let this be happening.* "But . . . why?" she finally whispered.

"Don't you see?" Billy cried, showing emotion for the first time since Carrie had opened the door. "Someone has to run the shop. Without the shop my parents have no income. Evan can't do it, he's in the Air Force—"

"Why is Evan's being in the Air Force more important than your music?" Carrie asked.

"I can do music there if I have to," Billy said. "Evan can't move the Air Force."

Carrie just sat there. She couldn't think of what to say. *I won't cry,* she vowed. *Billy needs me to be strong now.* She took a deep breath and pulled Billy into her arms. "It's going to be okay, Billy," she told him.

Billy pulled back and stared at her, pain etched over his face. "Come with me!"

"How can I?" Carrie asked. "I can't leave the kids—"

"Can't you find someone else for them to stay with?" he asked.

"You know I can't do that," Carrie said. "I have a commitment—"

"We have a commitment, too!" Billy cried.

"Believe me, I want to be with you!" Carrie said passionately. "I love you, and nothing is going to change that."

"I know," Billy said. He wiped his hand over his face again. "I don't know what I'm saying. I don't know what I'm doing . . ."

"Billy, everything will be okay," Carrie insisted. "You'll just be home for a little while. The band will wait for you. You know I'll wait for you. And then you'll come back here, where you belong—"

Billy stared at her, and a tear slid down his cheek. "I'm scared," he whispered.

Carrie gathered him into her arms. "It's okay, Billy," she crooned, "it's going to be okay. . . ."

She only prayed she was telling the truth.

TWELVE

"How soon do we have to leave?" Erin asked Carrie.

Carrie looked at her watch through eyes that felt gritty with exhaustion. "In about ten minutes," she replied.

It was early the next morning, and everyone was over at the Flirts' house, gathered in the living room. Billy was in his bedroom, packing. Since Claudia and Graham weren't back yet, Carrie had called her friend Darcy Laken, quickly explained the situation, and asked her if she could stay with Ian and Chloe for a couple of hours while she took Billy to the airport. Darcy had readily agreed.

"I just can't believe this is happening," Jay said, staring down at his own hands.

"First Sly and now this. The Flirts are breaking up."

"That's not true," Pres said sharply. "Billy will be back before you know it."

Silence filled the room. No one could look Pres in the eye. Billy had been totally straight with everyone. He didn't know when he'd be back. He didn't even know if he'd be back.

"What if he's not?" Jay asked in a low voice.

"He'll be back," Pres said in a steely voice.

"How many gigs do we cancel before we know?" Jay pressed nervously.

"I don't know!" Pres exploded. "Cut me a little slack here! This just happened."

Sam, who had been pacing the room, went to sit next to Pres on the shabby couch. She put her arms around him for moral support.

"The Flirts mean everything to Billy," Carrie said, "you guys know that." *And me,* she added in her own mind. *I mean everything to him. How can I stand this?*

"You and Billy can write while he's away," Jake suggested to Pres, rubbing the new stubble on his chin. "And, you know, tape stuff and send it back and forth . . ."

Pres just looked at him, then looked away.

"Look," Carrie began, "for Billy's sake, let's try to be upbeat when he comes out here, okay?"

"He'll know that's a lie," Emma said softly.

"We have to be strong for him now," Carrie insisted. "We have to let him know that we're all waiting for him to come back, that we'll wait as long as we have to and nothing will change!"

Silence.

Billy came into the living room, carrying a large suitcase. He set it down in the middle of the room and looked around at everyone. "I feel like I'm at my own funeral," he said.

Carrie went to him and put her hands on both sides of his face. "There's not going to be any funeral," she said, staring into his eyes as if she could will what she said to be true. "Your dad is going to get better, and then you're coming home to all of us."

Tears came to Billy's eyes, and he quickly blinked them back. He looked around at all his friends. "This does feel like home, man," he said gruffly.

"Because it is," Emma said. "Home is where people love you."

Billy took a deep ragged breath. "Yeah, well, enough of this stuff, or I'll never make it to the airport. Who's driving the van?"

"That'd be me," Jake said, dangling the keys from his finger.

"Let's go, then," Billy said. He took one last look around the living room. "Funny," he said softly. "Usually I just think about how funky this room is, and how we don't have any money to fix it up, but right now it looks just about perfect to me."

And on that note they all got into the van and headed for the ferry. Which would take them to the mainland. Where an expressway would lead them to the airport.

Where Billy will fly away, Carrie

thought, her heart clutching painfully. *Maybe forever.*

"Good morning, ladies and gentlemen," came the polished voice over the airport's P.A. system. "We would now like to begin preboarding at Gate 11C for American Flight 374 to Chicago, with continuing service to Seattle, Washington. Anyone who needs extra assistance boarding, or anyone traveling with small children, is invited to board at this time. . . . "

Billy turned to his friends, who stood around him in a semicircle. "This is really hard—"

"We're gonna miss you, man," Jake said.

"Hey, you'll be back before we even know it, right?" Jay said. "And we won't have to fight with you over the last beer in the fridge—"

Slowly Billy went around to each and every one of them, hugging them close, saying good-bye. Emma, Sam, and Erin were all crying. The guys kept trying to control themselves.

"This ain't good-bye," Pres said, his lip trembling. "You know I don't believe that."

"I don't know what it is," Billy said. "I have to take care of my family—"

"But just remember," Pres said, "you have to take care of yourself, too."

Billy and Pres stared at each other, then they embraced as if they never wanted to let go. Finally Pres pulled away. He turned away from Billy.

Slowly Billy walked over to Carrie and took her hand. Together they walked a few feet away from everyone else and stood in a corner together.

I will not cry, Carrie told herself. *I will be strong.* "I'm gonna miss you," she whispered. "No one makes me laugh the way you do."

"Well, I'll just save up my best jokes and deliver them to you on the phone at four A.M., how'll that be?" Billy asked, trying for levity. The depth of pain in his eyes gave him away. "How can I wake up in the morning and not know when I'm going to see you again?" he whispered.

"It'll be soon," Carrie promised. "I'll be here, waiting."

"For how long?" Billy asked.

"Forever," Carrie vowed.

Billy grabbed her and held her tight. "I love you so much."

"Ladies and gentlemen, this is your final boarding call for American Flight 374 to Chicago, with continuing service to Seattle, Washington . . ."

I have to memorize everything about this moment, Carrie thought, *the way he feels and looks and smells. All I want to do is scream "don't leave me!" but I can't. I can't!*

Billy pulled away from her gently and looked into her eyes. "If my dad doesn't get better—"

"He will," Carrie said firmly.

"But if he doesn't," Billy continued, "I want you to come to Seattle."

"Please, don't think about that now—"

"I can't help it," Billy said. "I need you to know how I feel. I . . . I can't make it without you—"

He grabbed her again and held her for the very last time. Slowly, he kissed her lips.

"I love you, Billy," she whispered. "I'll love you forever."

He smiled at her sadly, and traced the one tear that had fallen onto her cheek with the pad of his thumb. And then, with one last look into her eyes, he was gone.

Carrie stared listlessly out the window as the beautiful tree-lined streets of Sunset Island whizzed past them. They were back on the island. No one had said much of anything on the trip back. They had gotten as far as agreeing to cancel the gig they had in Bangor the following weekend. Other than that, they would just have to wait and see.

She still hadn't allowed herself to cry. It was as if she had worked so hard to be strong while Billy was still there, that now she couldn't let herself go.

I just can't believe he's gone, she thought as they passed Wheels, and the Cheap Boutique, and all the familiar spots where she and Billy had gone together. *Tuesday was the most wonderful day of my life, and today my entire life has fallen apart.*

The words to an old song her mom

used to sing when she was cooking—
something by Joni Mitchell—played over
and over in her head; a song about not
knowing what you have until it's gone.

"Carrie?" Emma said, touching her
shoulder lightly. "Do you have to get
right back to the Templetons'?"

Carrie shrugged. "Darcy said she could
stay as long as I needed her to."

Sam came over and knelt next to Carrie. "Listen, Erin is going to visit her dad
at the hospital, but Emma and I were
just thinking that maybe the three of us
could take a walk on the beach together.
What do you think?"

"Sure, I guess," Carrie said vaguely.

"I'll tell Jake," Emma said, and she
went up to the front of the van.

Soon Jake turned the van toward the
beach, stopping near the boardwalk not
far from the south end dunes.

"Thanks," Emma said, climbing out of
the van.

"Hey, we were thinking, maybe next
Sunday ya'll could come over to our
house," Pres said. "Hell, I'll cook up some

barbecue, and we can all call Billy together. . . . "

"That sounds great!" Sam said, forcing herself to sound enthusiastic. "Doesn't it sound great, Carrie?"

"Sure," Carrie replied dully. She began to climb out of the van, then she turned back to Jake. "Oh, thanks for the ride."

Pres reached out for Carrie's arm. "Listen, you know I'm here for you, girl, any hour of the day or night."

Carrie nodded.

"You call me, you hear?"

She nodded again.

Carrie closed the door and Jake pulled away.

"You know, you may not believe this," Sam said, "but cotton candy really does cure anything." She pulled Carrie toward the same cotton-candy stand she always seemed to frequent and ordered three cones, then handed one to each of her friends.

"Go ahead, fill yourself with empty, meaningless calories," Sam urged Carrie. "It's good for you."

Like some kind of automaton, Carrie

plucked off some of the pink spun sugar and stuck it in her mouth.

"Good, huh?" Sam urged.

"Sure," Carrie said in a flat voice.

The three of them walked slowly down the boardwalk, Sam gobbling her cotton candy, Emma and Carrie simply holding theirs. When Sam finished hers, she reached for Emma's and nervously started in on that one.

"Look, Billy will be back," Sam finally said.

Carrie sighed. "That's what I keep telling myself," she said. "But then another voice in my head whispers, 'maybe not.'"

"Pres told me Billy never got along all that well with his parents," Emma said.

Sam looked at her sharply. "When did Pres tell you that?"

Emma shook her head at Sam. "I don't remember. What difference does it make?"

"It doesn't," Sam said quickly, "it doesn't at all." She threw her empty cone into a nearby trash receptacle and reached for Carrie's. Her friend handed it to her automatically.

"Billy told me his parents didn't want

him to be a musician," Carrie said. "I think he still feels guilty about it." She sighed. "According to Billy, his older brother, Evan, is the 'good son.' I think Billy feels that he has to prove something to his parents—"

"That's he's a 'good son,' too," Emma put in.

Carrie nodded. "I'm afraid he'll put his whole life on hold to do whatever they need done. Even if it means putting his life on hold forever."

"He loves you, Carrie," Emma said fervently. "And he loves the band—"

"He asked me to go to Seattle," Carrie said.

"What?" Sam cried.

"If his dad doesn't get better," Carrie explained.

"But . . . but what about the Flirts?" Sam asked. "And Yale in the fall?"

Carrie sighed. "I don't know," she said heavily. "I just don't know."

"Let's walk out on the sand, okay?" Emma suggested.

Wordlessly they took off their sandals and left the boardwalk. The farther they walked, the less crowded the beach got. Here the water was choppy, there was no swimming allowed, and soon the sound of the surf was louder than the sound of humans.

"It's funny, isn't it?" Carrie finally said. "One minute your life can be so wonderful, and the next it can be so awful." She gave a small laugh. "I was so smug. I thought how much better my love life was than the two of yours." She turned to Sam. "You with all of your ups and downs with Pres." She turned to Emma. "And you with all your problems with Adam and Kurt. Well, I was certainly the dummy, wasn't I?"

"Carrie, being apart isn't going to hurt you and Billy," Emma said. "I really believe that."

"That's what you said once about you and Kurt," Carrie reminded her sadly. "You said even if you went to the Peace Corps in Africa, nothing could change your love for each other. But it turned out that even the *thought* of it changed everything."

"Kurt and I had a *lot* of problems,"

Emma said. "Not just that. You and Billy don't."

Carrie hummed the melody of the Joni Mitchell song, which still kept running over and over in her head.

"That's how I felt about Pres when I lost him," Sam said, referring to the song's lyrics.

"That's how I feel right now," Carrie said.

"Me, too," Emma admitted. She looked over at Sam. "I was wrong to get involved with Adam, Sam, because the truth of the matter is, I've never gotten over Kurt. And I don't know if I ever will."

Carrie shivered, even though the day was warm. "Billy's gone and Kurt's gone. It just feels so . . ."

"I want everything to be how it used to be!" Sam cried. "I mean, I can't stand this! Remember when the three of us were first falling for Billy and Pres and Kurt? Remember how great everything was?"

"That was then, this is now," Carrie said sadly.

"Well, I hate that!" Sam yelled. "I want all three guys here, right this minute! I want a . . . a big bonfire. With a lot of music. I want it to be the very beginning of a summer that's never, ever going to end. . . ."

The three of them climbed the far dune, stopping at the very top to look out at the glorious ocean.

"Guess what, Sam?" Carrie said sadly. "There's no going back. There's only going forward."

"Well, that just sucks—" Sam began.

Just at that moment Emma took in her breath sharply. She was facing away from the ocean, toward the valley between the dunes. Carrie and Sam followed her gaze to find out what had shocked her so much.

Standing there, looking up at them, was Kurt Ackerman.

"Am I dreaming?" Emma asked.

Carrie grabbed her hand. "Not unless we're all having the same dream."

Slowly the three girls walked down the sandy hill, and slowly Kurt walked toward them.

"Hi," he said softly, his eyes on Emma.

"Hi," she said, staring back at him. "I can't believe you're here," Emma breathed.

"We seem to meet only on the beach," Kurt said, his eyes boring into hers.

"It doesn't seem real," Emma said, gulping hard. She laughed a short, breathy laugh. "It's just as you imagined it in your letter—"

"Except you were supposed to be wearing a white dress . . ." Kurt said.

"Maybe now we can conjure up Pres, and Billy, too," Sam joked, still staring in awe at Kurt, at the fact that he was really there.

He looked at her and raised his eyebrows in question. And then Sam quickly told him what had happened.

Kurt turned to Carrie. "I'm so sorry," he said.

She nodded, unable to speak.

Then slowly Kurt put out his arms, and the next thing Carrie knew she was in them, along with Sam and Emma. All four of them were hugging one another, crying at the same time. For Carrie it was as if a dam broke and she finally let out all the tears she had been saving since Billy had told her the terrible news about his father.

"You came back," Emma whispered to Kurt through her tears.

"Yeah," Kurt said. He turned to Carrie and kissed her on the forehead. "And Billy will, too."

Sam laughed and brushed the tears off her face. "Maybe we *can* go back, Carrie!"

"No," Carrie managed to say, "we'll go forward. Together. And we'll just have to pray that's enough."

SUNSET ISLAND MAILBOX

Dear Readers,

Getting mail from all of you is one of the very best parts of writing the <u>Sunset Island</u> books. And the photos—too cool! You'll find that I really do try to give serious consideration to your thoughts and book ideas. For example, I received a lot of mail asking me to tackle issues like AIDS, teen pregnancy, and date rape in a <u>Sunset</u> book. The AIDS issue comes up in <u>Sunset Heart</u> and you'll find that the issue of teen pregnancy is addressed in an upcoming book as well. So please keep those letters coming. Your ideas mean so much to me! As always, let me know if I can consider your letter for publication.

I got a letter a few months ago from Claire Gunselman, who lives just outside of Chicago. Claire said that her dream was to meet me. I wrote her back and told her that if she was ever in Nashville, I would be happy to take her to lunch. Well, Claire called me up and said her parents would bring her to Nashville. Are her parents cool, or what? We had a great lunch together. She is darling, and smart, and funny, and I predict the world will hear big things from her.

To Jenni Sarna of Dale City, Virginia, and Whitney Guy of Pottstown, Pennsylvania, and everyone else who has asked me to write faster . . . I'm writing as fast as I can! To Christle Moreland, Amy Myrrh Leonard, Samantha Raines, and Lori Rae Nelson, and all the rest of you incredible girls from Iola, Kansas— thanks for all your enthusiasm and support! I get tons of letters from Iola—I really want to visit you guys some time! My favorite reader's name of the month . . . Bridgett Miracle!

As always, thank you for reading my books, and for sharing your lives with me. It's an honor. Let me leave you with one final thought. This week, try to do one spontaneous act of kindness. If you have time, write and let me know what you did! You're the greatest!

See you on the island!
Best-
Cherie Bennett

Cherie Bennett
c/o General Licensing Company
24 West 25th Street
New York, New York 10010.

Dear Cherie,
Hi! I just received your letter and I really like it. I think it's great that you answer all your mail. Do you ever get any hate mail? Also, I think you should put a picture of Jeff with you in a book. I'd really like to know what he looks like!

Thanks,
Meredith Gilbert
Winchester, Massachusetts

Dear Meredith

Once I did a call-in radio talk show here in Nashville, and evidently some of the things I said were controversial, because I received some hate mail and phone calls after that. It was really scary. I've never gotten hate mail from a reader, though sometimes there are strong suggestions of things I should do or should not do in a future Sunset book. It's a great idea about Jeff's picture, although I think my publisher would nix the idea. Anyway, Jeff is six feet tall, slender and muscular, with brown eyes and a ponytail. I think he's darling, but what's more important is that he is an incredible guy, and my favorite person in the entire world.

Best,
Cherie

Dear Cherie,
I'm writing to tell you about the covers of the books. It looks as if you've had trouble finding someone to model as Sam and Emma recently. The Emma on the cover of Sunset Wedding *and* Sunset Glitter *has to go! I love your books, and tell Jeff I say hey!*

Your biggest fan from Georgia,
Janie Hays
Woodstock, Georgia

Dear Janie,
Believe it or not, the Emma model hasn't changed since the very beginning! It's just that after four years her hair had gotten longer and she's changed a little. You've probably changed a bit yourself in that amount of time! Carrie is the same, too. Be sure to look for a new and improved Sam on all the recent books, including Sunset Sensation (out in June), Sunset Magic (July), Sunset Illusions, Sunset Fire (September), Sunset Fantasy (October), and Sunset Passion (November).

Best,
Cherie

Dear Cherie,

My cousin Niki and I think you are an outstanding author. We're reading all your books. They are by far the best teen books ever written. Can you please send us two autographed pictures of yourself?

Your readers,
Lisa Perrella and Niki Holmes
Whitestone, New York

Dear Lisa and Niki,

I love the idea of two cousins reading <u>Sunset</u> books together. I get a lot of letters from best friends who read about Carrie, Sam, and Emma's adventures together, too. To all of you who have written me asking for an autographed picture, I'm really sorry but I literally get thousands of requests, so I just can't do it. I'm thinking of starting a fan club, and if I do you'll get an autographed picture when you join. I promise to keep you all posted on this. As for my picture, you can find a photo in the back of every book (although now my hair is long and blond), which was taken by my good buddy David Frohman.

Best,
Cherie